COMFORTLESS MEMORY

COMFORTLESS MEMORY

by

Maurice Baring

Dales Large Print Books
Long Preston, North Yorkshire,
BD23 4ND, England.

British Library Cataloguing in Publication Data.

Baring, Maurice
    Comfortless memory.

      A catalogue record of this book is
      available from the British Library

      ISBN   978-1-84262-569-9 pbk

First published in Great Britain in 1928

Copyright © The Trustees of the Maurice Baring Will Trust

Cover illustration by arrangement with
P.W.A. International Ltd.

The right of Maurice Baring to be identified as the author of
this work has been asserted

Published in Large Print 2008 by arrangement with
A P Watt Literary, Film & Television Agents

Dales Large Print is an imprint of Library Magna Books Ltd.

Printed and bound in Great Britain by
T.J. (International) Ltd., Cornwall, PL28 8RW

To
LL

PREFACE

The author of this story left it in his will. It was to be published after his death. He wrote it, so he said, partly to explain his conduct to a friend who played an important part in the drama he relates, and partly as a warning to the well-meaning.

It was not, he said, in a letter he left with it, *Dichtung und Wahrheit* – not Truth *and* Fiction, but Truth.

He was referring to the essence of the story.

As to the circumstances, he changed much: the names, the dates, and sometimes the places.

The biography of the author has never been published; but if it were written, the following narrative would supply a missing fragment and an unguessed-of chapter.

So far as our story approaches the end,
Which do you pity…?

ROBERT BROWNING

'and left
Memory comfortless.'

ROBERT LYTTON

CHAPTER 1

I was *'nel mezzo del cammin di nostra vita,'* and beyond it, when an unexpected success upset the tenor of my life.

Someone once said that when a man starts out to write his *magnum opus* he nearly always makes a mess of it. So it happens conversely that the best works of authors are often the offspring of a careless moment, of a period of leisure, fun or recreation.

A trifle that an artist whose work has hitherto been serious and solid threw off in a holiday mood may sometimes turn out to be his masterpiece. Cervantes wrote *Don Quixote* to beguile the tedium of his prison hours, and possibly Shakespeare wrote some of his finest passages at the bidding of an importunate actor who thought his part was too short.

However that may be, after years of patient, slender labour, relative obscurity, respectful recognition and limited remuneration in the world of letters, and to a certain extent in the larger world, I sent my publisher a modern novel – a kind of fantasy, half-serious, half-flippant, in rhyme, which I had written during a brief holiday in Torquay.

He was doubtful about publishing it. He thought it a daring novelty, but a wrong note in the rather drab serious scheme of my work. He feared it would damage my reputation with the serious public. I insisted, wishing to get rid of the thing; as someone else said, all works of art are after all only sheddings. The book was published, and it had more than a success. The public went mad about it, and not only the English, but the European, public.

It came at the right time. The two main characters in the story appealed to, caught, and perhaps represented the mood of the moment. It was dramatized, made into a play and an operetta; the names of the hero and the heroine were given to hats and racehorses and dishes and pens and railway engines. It was translated into every European language and even into Chinese and Japanese.

All this created a temporary demand for my serious work and stirred up a whirlwind of dust about my quiet life. Teresa, my wife, and I were importuned by the attendant sprites of notoriety and popularity. Work, serious work, became impossible, and I was halfway through what, if it was not to be a *magnum opus*, was a conscientious and serious attempt which necessitated uninterrupted thought and steady application.

At home there was no more peace. So we settled to go abroad for a year, until the storm – and such storms are short-lived – blew over: to Italy. Our son was at a public school, and we thought it would be a good thing for him to learn Italian in his holidays.

We left England in autumn and arrived at Rome in November, and stayed there first at an hotel and then in a flat until February. Thence in February we migrated to Naples, where we took a villa.

At Rome I made the acquaintance of Charles Donne, the artist. I had seen pictures of his exhibited in Paris and in London ... he was still a young man, although he had said goodbye to the enchanted age of twenty-five. He was just beginning to make a name, and he was spending a year in Italy working at various pictures.

We were both of us swept away by his personality: his enthusiasm, his impetuousness, his fun and his confiding friendliness, and, above all, his talent. His talent showed in everything he said and did. He was at this period not only young, but young for his age. He not only introduced us to works of art and to places, but to people – the kind of people we wanted to know.

Teresa and I got to know him very well and very quickly. The rapidity with which his friendship with myself and his intimacy with both of us grew up, although we took it for granted at the time, seems to me now, on looking back on it, surprising.

We had determined to make no friends in Rome, and he took us by storm; in a week's time we felt as if we had known him for years. We met first, of course, on the common ground of art. His interest in my work was great, if not greater, than mine in his: Teresa and I had a well-justified belief in his powers; we were longing for him to be better known and to do more; we expected great things of him; but apart from art and work, and wishes for his success, he very soon became indispensable to us both as a friend and to me as a companion.

I found he understood everything without being told. That although apparently he looked at nothing, he saw everything, and that he lighted firmly on the best. He gave me a sense of understanding which at times Teresa's comments, and still more her silences, failed to give me. Teresa liked him as much as I did. I think that she liked him more than she admired him; while I admired him even more than I liked him. He knew Rome well ... and as it was the first time Teresa and I had been to Italy, we found in him a heaven-sent guide.

The notoriety of my popular work had reached Rome. It had appeared in the Tauchnitz edition, and the operetta taken from it, and set to music by a brilliant and famous French composer, was being performed both in Milan and in Rome; but this work, like all my other books, had been published under a pseudonym, and nobody suspected that the rather serious middle-aged Englishman and his Austrian wife ('we never dreamt he was married,' they would have said) was 'Lawrence Jeremy', the author of the *Silver Pound* (called in French *Le Liard d'or*) which was setting so many young heads a-dreaming and so many old heads a-nodding.

Charles Donne was insistent on our seeing Naples, but he was too busy to go there with us before February, and we were contented where we were, so we did not think of moving until February, when we heard that a comfortable villa owned by an Englishman was to let. We took it and persuaded

Charles Donne to come with us. We kept our flat in Rome.

The weather was fine. The house was comfortable; the Italian servants warm and welcoming. We made expeditions; there was time for work and the right kind of recreation. Charles found he could work better at Naples than in Rome; and he began a portrait of Teresa – which promised well: he had caught her stately lines and the softness in her eyes. All was for the best in the most beautiful of worlds. We made no new acquaintances, except a few artist friends of Charles'.

We had not been at Naples a fortnight, before one morning Teresa, while she was out shopping, met an old friend of hers in the street.

This was Jenny True, the daughter of an Englishman who had occupied for years a minor official position – a man of culture, and well-known in English society. Teresa had been at the same convent, and afterwards at the same *pension*, in Paris as Jenny True. Jenny was the greatest friend of her youth.

Jenny had married when she was only eighteen a young and penniless officer in a cavalry regiment. Her father had died some years before, and he would certainly have delayed if not prevented the marriage. Her mother was a pretty and amiable French-woman, whose desire was to please (she could not say 'No' to anyone) and she thought the match perfect.

Jenny and her husband went to India. A baby was born, and died. Four years later, her husband died of fever. She came back from India to London, and there she made the acquaintance of a certain Sir J– D–, a financier, who was older than she was – a man of brains and talent, but delicate in health; one of his lungs was affected.

He fell madly in love with Jenny, but he could not marry her as he had a wife already who was shut up in a lunatic asylum, and as divorce was impossible, they lived together as man and wife without bothering about formalities or convention.

Sir J– was at the zenith of a successful career when his health broke down, and he was obliged to live abroad. They tried various places: Cannes, Madeira, the Canary Islands. They finally settled at Naples, where they lived for the greater part of the year, paying brief visits to Rome and sometimes to Paris.

After they had lived together for five years, Sir J– died, leaving Jenny all his money and his villa at Naples.

This happened a year before we went to Italy. I had only seen Jenny True once or twice: just after her marriage and just before mine.

I remember in every detail the morning when Teresa arrived with the news that she had met Jenny True.

It was cold and damp. It had rained a little. I had spent the morning wandering about the town. I had dawdled near a blacksmith's watching him at work... I strayed into a church, where a ragged, mixed crowd were assisting at a requiem... I bought some flowers... I strolled home, and the first thing that Teresa said to me was, 'Jenny True is here.'

At first I hardly remembered who Jenny True was; then in a moment it came back to me, and I said mechanically:

'We must ask her to luncheon or dinner.'

'She has asked us,' Teresa said, 'next Wednesday, and I said we could go.'

'What about Charles?'

'Charles hates going out to dinner, so I said nothing about him,' said Teresa; and I remember thinking at that moment that Teresa did not wish Charles to meet Jenny. I said nothing. We went to dinner with Jenny

True on the following Wednesday. Charles was dining with an artist friend.

I was interested at seeing Jenny True again, for, although I had not seen her for so long, I had heard a great deal about her. She was a person whose name was in italics. Nobody during the last few years could have gone to the South of France or to Italy without hearing about her. It was said she was beautiful, and attractive ... and the wildest tales were told about her by those who live on the fringe of all societies. It was said by some that she had lovers by the score, that she was a dangerous, wicked, unscrupulous woman; by others that she was much maligned, simple, natural and sensible, a victim to her great good nature.

Her looks, too, were discussed, although it was admitted that she had something, even by those who could 'see nothing' in her.

We dined with her at her villa. It was far larger than ours, and done up and arranged with exquisite taste. It looked as if it had not been changed since the days of Lady Hamilton. Whether this was due to Jenny or to Sir J– I don't know; and the evidence was conflicting. The men said Jenny had wonderful taste; the women that Sir J– had done it all, and that Jenny was quick at assimilating...

There was a large party: some Italians who seemed greatly at their ease and at home in the Casa D–, an old friend, Mrs Sedley; a French journalist, an American, Mr Tiffany, whom we had met in London, and his wife, and a Captain Harris, a middle-aged English ex-soldier who was good-looking, cosmopolitan, and had been everywhere and knew everybody. He gave one the vague impression of being the unofficial master of the house.

As for Jenny herself, she was dressed in black, with a tulle scarf round her neck, which suited her great fairness and her light blue, laughing eyes and, whatever anyone else might think, I thought her ravishingly graceful and attractive. I longed for someone to paint her.

She was friendly and engaging, and seemed to give all she had to give with both hands. She was gay on the surface, with a hidden background of sadness, and she pervaded the room like a silvery mist.

The next morning Teresa and I were drinking our coffee on the verandah. Charles was not there; he was already at work. I remembered there was an article about a book of mine in *The Times* that reached us that morning, and I asked Teresa if she had read it.

She said: 'No, dear, I haven't seen *The Times*.'

I was disappointed, and showed it.

'You see,' she said very gently, 'you always take *The Times*,' as she poured out the coffee. (Teresa never read newspapers.) I then said:

'We must ask Jenny True to dinner.'

We discussed the day and the guests.

I said: 'Charles must be here, of course,' and Teresa said:

'Charles can dine out; he hates meeting people ... except his own artist friends.'

The dialogue proceeded thus:

'I think he would like to meet Jenny.'

'I don't think Charles would like to get entangled with Jenny's surroundings.'

'Are they so different from ours and his?'

'Charles is very naive and modest – and still very young for his age.'

'All the better ... that's the reason why I want him to be there ... in spite of his Quartier Latin experience, he is still unripe, still insular and rusty, and the sooner he rubs off that rust the better. He ought to have a great career before him ... only he doesn't know the world, and he must get to know it.'

Teresa at once quoted Goethe. She was prone to do that: the celebrated lines about talent being formed by stillness, but character in the stream of the world.

'But a great artist must have character,' I objected, 'as well as talent. Goethe proved the contrary of his precept by the example of his practice.'

'It would have been better for Goethe's talent if he hadn't,' she said.

'The more an artist is a man of the world the better,' I answered. Teresa smiled. Perhaps she was pitying me. I returned to the charge.

'If Charles is to be a great portrait painter, as I hope and think he will be, he must know human nature. He must know the world. He *must* make it his oyster.'

'I'm afraid he'll cut his fingers with the knife.'

'We all do that more or less; don't think I am giving the world more than its due.'

I remember quoting Goethe to her:

'...Kenn' Ich doch
Die Welt von Jugend auf, wie sie so leicht
Uns hülflos, einsam lässt, und ihren Weg
Wie Sonn' und Mond und andre Götter
    geht.'

I said that Goethe knew life and estimated the world at its true value, but he knew there was no escape from it. The point was, to get the better of the world. However worthless one thinks the game, one must win and not lose. In other words, you must be a master or a slave. 'Charles,' I said, 'has the makings of a master.'

Teresa said I was talking as if Charles was to be a man of action and not an artist. He was not going, she said, into the business world; I was talking as if he had a career in American finance before him. She quoted all the great artists who had failed from a worldly point of view and whose work had gained rather than suffered from it: Shelley, Bizet, Millet. They had been slaves. They had gone under.

I said that failure from the worldly point of view, failure in the art and conduct of life, might often happen to be the price an artist paid for his success in his art – sometimes a posthumous success – but it did not always follow that a ruined life meant good art, and that good art was sometimes the fruit of a serene and well-managed life, and I quoted Goethe... I said this was especially true of painters, and I quoted Leonardo da Vinci... She did not want Charles to make havoc of his life.

She caught me up there.

'That's just it,' she said. 'I don't think Jenny would be a good friend for Charles.'

I pooh-poohed the idea of Charles falling a prey to Jenny: she was not his type at all, and her life was full.

'Jenny,' said Teresa – and I remember her words as if she had said them yesterday – 'has a fatal gift of intimacy with almost everyone she meets... And Charles is so susceptible.'

I contested the idea of Charles being attracted by Jenny. What I said sounded plausible at the time!

Charles had hitherto been attracted more by artistic beauty, by artists' beauty, than by ordinary feminine grace ... he had admired the exotic, the rare, the bizarre ... or else the forcible, the original ... an enigmatic expression, a fantastic colouring, a striking outline... He had less eye for the essentially feminine refinements and graces.

La Bruyère said that you must judge a woman from the heels of her shoes to the crown of her coiffure, just as you measure a fish from head to tail. Now this was the whole point of Jenny True ... her feminine completeness ... her intangible grace. I couldn't imagine Charles, or, indeed, anyone else, painting her.

Teresa admitted this, but she said that

Jenny had something more dangerous than all that, quite outside the region of what was paintable or not.

I said, 'What?' She couldn't define it. She said it was her manner, her 'being', her *'Wesen'* ... a *'holder Leichtsinn'*. She asked me to translate that.

I couldn't. I suggested, 'a lovely frivolity', or a 'divine frivolity'.

Then I argued that if he did fall in love with Jenny, it was no great matter. It would be a liberal education for him. Far better than if he fell in love with a sordid model. He was sure to fall in love with someone.

Teresa said that she felt responsible for Charles. We had brought him to Naples. I, who knew his father, knew well, she said, that he wouldn't like Charles to become an appanage of Jenny's world.

Then I became irritated. I said that Charles' father was a Philistine, and that Charles wasn't a baby. He'd lived in Paris and Rome, and in the Bohemian world at that...

'That's all quite different,' she said. 'He has lived among people, however sordid and lax in morals, who are artists and workers. But Jenny's world is a world of wasters and wastrels – wasps, not bees – a disintegrating, idle world. It's his work I'm afraid of – not his morals.'

She laid stress on Jenny's friends, her milieu, the kind of people we had met at her house... That was the kind of people with whom Jenny was always surrounded wherever she lived.

'I'm not saying anything against Jenny,' she said. 'Her life is her own affair, but I don't think I would choose that kind of surroundings for my son, especially if I wished him to work hard.'

I said there was no reason Charles should make friends with Jenny's friends. It was most unlikely.

'Jenny is deceptive,' Teresa said. 'She looks like a *nachtschmetterling* – a soft, silver moth – but she is really like a candle, she draws people into her flame.'

Then I very foolishly told her she was jealous; although I didn't really think so.

Teresa said quite truly that she was only jealous of the women I liked, and not always then. I knew this was true.

But instead of assenting, I said: 'I believe all women are jealous of Jenny True, and the better they are the more jealous they are.'

Teresa reminded me that I hardly knew Jenny, whereas she was one of her oldest friends.

I asked her satirically if she meant women were not jealous of their friends.

'I should be frightfully jealous of anyone you cared for,' she said, 'but I really think I am disinterested about Charles.'

I knew this was true, but I said:

'I'm not sure. I think you think he belongs to you.'

She told me I was absurd.

I made it worse, digging in my toes. The short dialogue that ensued is burnt into my mind.

'All women are the same,' I began.

Teresa laughed good-humouredly.

'You really think I could be jealous of Jenny because of Charles?'

'Yes, and I don't blame you ... I like you for it. You wouldn't be a woman if you weren't like that.'

Teresa laughed pityingly.

'My poor, dear child, how little you understand women!'

Then she gave in, and said she would certainly ask Charles. Then I gave in and said perhaps we had better not.

'I think,' I added, 'you are right about his work, and if he meets her, let it be by chance.'

But Teresa became obstinate in her turn

and repeated to me the arguments I had used against her.

'He must face the world – all worlds. I will ask him directly he comes down.'

I begged her not to. I said I had only been joking. She insisted, and the discussion was cut short by Charles coming in himself.

He drank his coffee. The matter was not mentioned until Teresa said to me: 'We haven't told Charles about our dinner party.'

I asked Charles to dinner; and walked into the garden. I took *The Times* with me to read it quietly.

CHAPTER 2

Our dinner party came off. We asked such of Jenny's friends as we knew.

Captain Harris... Countess Zikov, a Russian... Hedworth Adderly, an ex-artist ... and Jane Sedley.

Charles sat between Jane and Countess Zikov; Jenny True sat next to me.

Teresa's remark about Jenny looking like a soft, silver moth came into my mind. She was dressed in black tulle and silver.

Jenny True spilt a wineglass full of water at the beginning of dinner, and caught Charles' eye as she did it. She laughed, a quick, rippling, piteous laugh which seemed to say, 'Don't you laugh, too, or I shall never be able to stop.'

'It's too dreadful,' she said. 'I am so, so sorry.'

I was in the middle of what I thought was a picturesque description of the Dalmatian coast, and I remember being faintly put out. I didn't want to laugh at that moment.

After dinner we all went out together in the Italian fashion, but the men had their coffee in the smoking-room, and then we mingled.

Teresa suggested music.

Hedworth Adderly played the popular tunes of the moment in all languages, humming the words. He played by ear, and his repertory was wide.

Jane said she hated all modern music, and Teresa said that Hedworth was full of talent and could play anything, but that nobody could write melody now... Adderly played a well-known Neapolitan air. It had reached the London music halls and barrel-organs, and had been hackneyed all over Europe beyond the limits of nausea. Teresa shuddered, and Jane shivered, and Harris looked pained, but I heard Jenny saying in a low voice to Charles:

'I love that tune.'

'So do I,' said Charles.

I asked Charles casually the next day what he thought of Jenny. His answer was characteristic.

'She's not my epoch ... she's Watteau ... but I thought her very easy to get on with.'

On the Sunday after our dinner party, Jane Sedley came to see us. Charles had gone to Rome on business for a day or two.

Jane Sedley was an old friend. She had started life as an artist, had won the *prix de Rome*, and now she supported herself and her only daughter Mabel, who was grown up, by illustrating novels and stories in the magazines. Her husband, who had been a dramatic critic, was dead.

She generally spent the winter abroad with her daughter. She was large, solid and comfortable. Her father was Scottish, and people said she must have Spanish blood to account for her dark hair and piercing eyes.

However that might be, she was practical; she looked at life steadily and could abide no nonsense; people liked her, and she was a mine of personal information.

She talked of Jenny True. She knew her well.

'It's after all a comfort that that old bore, Sir J– is dead. I thought he would never die.'

Teresa said Jenny was very fond of him.

She shrugged her shoulders.

'Oh! fond of him – yes. I suppose you are fond of a person to whom you sacrifice your life and your reputation and everything you've got ... but ... but well, she made the best of it. He left her everything. She will be very well off ... the sisters are furious, of course.'

We discussed Jenny True; her past and her present and her future, until she herself arrived. She had, I remember, a fur boa round her neck and a bunch of white violets pinned somewhere. It was a fine spring day. She looked younger than when I had seen her before. We had tea. In the course of the conversation – Jenny was full of praise of our dinner; she had enjoyed it so much – Charles' name came up.

'I liked him so much,' said Jenny. 'He's not like an artist, at least not like the artists I know... He looks so clean and fresh ... tell me all about him.'

I obeyed, and, in order to make this story clear to the reader, I will repeat what I told

Jenny True that day.

Charles Donne was the son of a retired colonel who lived in Somersetshire. His mother had died when he was at school. He had been brought up by two hectoring aunts, and he had spent some of his childhood in India He was destined for the Army, and went to one of the smaller public schools which specialised in military aspirants; but from his earliest youth he had determined to be an artist. He asked his father to send him to the Slade School. His father refused. They had row after row, and quarrel after quarrel. Charles refused to go to Woolwich, and indeed, made it impossible by deliberately failing in his examination, which he could have passed easily, as he had a turn for mathematics. His father refused to send him to a university on the plea that he could not afford it. Charles then asked to be allowed to go to the Quartier Latin to study art. The aunts held up their hands in pious horror ... but at last, largely owing to the influence of a wise master who had been Charles' tutor at school, he was allowed to go. He went to Paris, and he studied there for five years under Ducros. Ducros said he had real talent as well as a definite vocation, and prophesied great things of him. He came back to

London. A picture of his was hung in the Grosvenor Gallery. It attracted attention. The next year he exhibited again, and his work was praised by Henry Howard, the critic, whose word was at that time law among the artistic. He was very poor – his father allowed him the smallest possible pittance, and his life was a desperate struggle until he received an important order for a portrait of the beautiful wife of a rich financier. The picture was exhibited – it was beautiful and new – and Charles from nobody became somebody in the world of art. He was reconciled with his father. He was given some orders ... not many, but too many for his taste... He left London and went to Italy for the first time. He had been a year in Italy when we arrived, and he had no intention of going home at present. He had painted nothing important since the picture of Mrs H–

When I had finished this narrative, Jane Sedley supplied the commentary.

'He is still,' she said, 'only a *promising* artist in spite of his achievement – which is something. His artistic fate is in the balance. He may do great things. He *ought* to do great things. On the other hand, he may remain an artist of promise all his life: the painter of one clever picture. The portrait of Mrs H–, is very striking, but he ought to do far better than that. Ducros told me himself he thought he was capable of going very far. Ducros was not satisfied with that portrait. He is still very young in his art ... and aggressive. He is still at the stage of saying to himself, 'This, of course, will shock you.' It doesn't shock us. We have seen it all twenty or thirty years ago. The young have always thought the same. But he ought to do well, unless ... unless it all comes to an end now.'

We asked her what she meant.

She looked at us with her piercing brown eyes, and said: 'I have guessed his secret.'

'What secret?' I asked.

'He is in love,' said Jane, 'in love with Alice Tiffany. I know it through Mabel, who is Alice's greatest friend. They were at the same *pension* at Dresden.'

'But where is the girl?' I asked. 'She wasn't there the other night.'

'She's gone to Rome to meet her father, and they're coming here at once. The girl is a beauty. Crystal clear, a divine complexion, wonderful features ... that fair, clear American type that is so fresh while it lasts, and fades so soon.'

'Is he really in love with her?' Teresa asked.

'Mabel,' said Jane, 'says he really is ... they

have been seeing a great deal of each other at Rome ... that he would never have come to Naples if he hadn't known the Tiffanys were coming here ... but she doesn't think he's proposed.'

'And the girl?' asked Jenny, with what I thought was a civil interest and nothing more.

Jane lowered her voice and became confidential, as was her habit.

'Mabel isn't sure. She says she likes him, but she's not sure whether she's in love with him. She's so young.'

'Surely,' said Jenny, 'it ought to do well. I expect they will be happy.'

'Happy, possibly,' said Jane, 'but I was thinking of his art ... artists oughtn't to be happy ... at any rate, they seldom are ... at least, not good artists ... and when they marry they are nearly always finished ... I know it from experience,' she sighed. 'There was a time when I thought I had wings that could fly to heaven ... then there's the butcher's book ... and the children's new boots ... but I daresay they will be happy. What do you think, Teresa?'

Teresa thought a little.

'I want Charles to be happy,' she said, 'art or no art; but perhaps I'm sentimental.'

'Then,' said Jane decidedly, 'you had better give up the idea of his being a great artist.'

'You think the two things are incompatible?' I asked.

Jane looked at me and laughed.

'There are exceptions,' she said, 'one at least. But I do think that if Charles is happy he won't paint any more.'

'I hope he will be happy,' said Jenny, 'and marry that nice girl. She sounds perfect.'

'We shall soon see,' said Jane.

Then we talked of other things.

When Jane went away, Jenny True stayed on, and we tried to persuade her to stay for dinner, but she was engaged. I left her with Teresa and went up to my room to work. They had a long talk. Teresa told me all about it afterwards. They talked about Charles, and the possibility of his marrying. Jenny then said that she thought marrying too young was the greatest mistake in the world. She said among other things, 'If I hadn't married so young, I think I could have kept straight.'

Teresa asked her if she would have listened if anyone had tried to prevent her marrying.

She said she didn't think so. If her father had been alive, he would probably have asked them to wait a year ... he was clever and full of tact ... she always did what he wanted in the end. He never insisted, or never seemed to insist on a point, and yet always got his way. Her mother had been hopeless about it. 'She couldn't refuse me anything.'

'It's a comfort,' said Jenny, 'that she is not alive to see the sequel; she wouldn't have understood and she was so good.'

Teresa asked her, of course, whether she was happy. It was a question she could never resist.

She said she was enjoying herself ... having fun ... that she liked her friends ... her house, she said, was like a club ... people dropped in every night after dinner, quantities of people of all sorts. She said she hadn't many women friends ... she didn't think she wanted any. She said everyone was so nice to her ... and so kind to her ... but she felt like someone in an old French play ... *Le Demi-Monde,* the play which started the word. It meant then something quite different from what it means now ... it meant people who looked all right, but who were just *outside* things – on the fringe ... *pêches à quinze sous* ... peaches which were quite perfect to look at and ... only, there was another basket of peaches next to them which were labelled *À trente sous* ... they looked just the same, why was one sort of peach half as dear? The *pêches à quinze sous* looked perfect, but every one of them had some slight spot or blemish ... a little spot of rot ... a little brown spot ... or a bruise ... and that's why they were cheaper ... that's why they were priced at *quinze sous* instead of at *trente sous*. You had to turn them round and look at them carefully to find the spot ... but it was there. Jenny said she was like the woman in that play. She belonged to the *demi-monde* in the old, old-fashioned, forgotten sense of the word ... only, there was no drama ... it didn't matter. She was not engaged in any intrigue. She didn't want to marry an innocent young man ... she would have told the young man everything to start with ... she didn't want to get anywhere ... or to be made an honest woman of ... perhaps the world had become different ... perhaps it liked dishonest women best. At any rate, everyone was charming to her – except people she didn't know and didn't want to know... She said that she was happy ... really quite happy... Teresa said that Jenny was laughing the whole time she made this confession, and that her laughter was so infectious that she made Teresa laugh, too.

I said to Teresa: 'Then she really is happy?'

'Happy?' said Teresa. 'My poor child!'

42

CHAPTER 3

On the following Sunday, Mrs Tiffany asked us to dinner at her hotel. She said her husband and her daughter would be there. Charles was invited as well.

Charles went out early in the morning ... he was going to spend the whole day somewhere painting ... we did not press for information, we thought very likely he was going for an expedition with the Tiffanys.

When it was time to dress for dinner, there was no sign of Charles. We thought he had forgotten, although we had reminded him, and he had said he would certainly not forget. We were just about to start without him when he arrived, breathless and flustered. He changed in about four minutes, and we arrived not overlate for dinner.

Mr Tiffany – Harold K Tiffany – was there, with his wife and his daughter Alice.

I was immensely struck by the daughter's appearance. I think I have seldom seen a more lovely, radiant creature. There was something diaphanous about her; something that reminded one of a dragonfly or a shell ... her complexion was too good, and had the slightly hectic bloom you see in consumptives ... her eyes were wide and grey ... her features exquisite ... but from the moment I talked to her, and I sat next to her and Jenny, I felt somehow not that she was not for Charles but that Charles was not for her ... she was assimilative, but, I felt, essentially matter of fact ... the kind of girl all other women would call stupid. I wondered whether, in the course of time, this radiant girl would grow to look like her mother, who was now all bone; hard, energetic and dry, with a skin like weather-beaten parchment, and something of an iron side about her, although she was not old.

I remember also wondering whether Alice would live long, or die like the heroine in one of Henry James' novels. One of my surmises was correct. I will say which one later on.

There were many guests, Italians and others. Charles sat next to Jane Sedley. After dinner we played cards. Charles and Miss Tiffany were left out, and they talked together for a time, until there was a shuffle and Charles was taken away to talk to an Italian lady, and Alice Tiffany was asked to sing. Her father, who was silver-haired, courteous, rather long-winded, and came from Virginia, asked her to sing a song called 'Jessie', of which the refrain was 'Although you can never be mine', but she said she could not sing that by heart, and she sang a popular American melody instead.

As we were leaving, Mrs Tiffany said to Charles: 'Don't forget you are dining with us on Wednesday.'

Before he could answer, her daughter said: 'Mr Donne can't come; he's got a date.'

'But it was arranged; he promised,' Mrs Tiffany said, peevishly. The girl interrupted her mother.

'No, mother dear, he didn't understand; it was my fault. I had told him it was all off – because you see I wasn't sure I'd be here...'

'It's a disappointment,' said Mrs Tiffany, 'but we must arrange something else now.'

I have related this little incident in detail because I believe it contained and hid a turning point in all our lives.

In the first place, Charles told us the reason he had been late was that he had missed the train from wherever he had been spending the day; he was walking in the village, having settled to drive back, when he met Jenny True in her carriage. She had been spending the day there too, with an aunt of hers who lived there. Jenny had offered him a lift home. It turned out, moreover, that the 'date' which prevented him from going to the Tiffanys was with Jenny.

During the next fortnight I was engrossed in a piece of work I was finishing, and I imagined Charles to be working too, but we seldom saw him.

He was always dining out, too, with his artist friends, as I thought.

I heard nothing of the Tiffanys or of Jenny True. Life had slipped back for me into its usual rut, after a swift gleam of social life.

Then one day Jane Sedley proposed herself to luncheon. Charles was, as usual, out for the day.

She waited till the coffee was brought on to the verandah, and we were comfortably smoking, to say:

'And what is Charles Donne doing?'

I remember saying, rather peevishly, that we seldom saw him now.

Jane's eyes sparkled with interest. 'I suppose he goes out a lot.'

I said that he was supposed to be painting a lot, out of doors, but we never saw any result. Teresa said it was only natural that we saw little of him, if he was in love with such a beautiful girl.

I lamented his idleness. He had done really nothing lately, I was convinced of it. However, I couldn't blame either him or Miss Tiffany.

Then Jane, who had prepared her effect, brought it out.

'It's not Alice,' she said.

We asked who it was.

Jane had the immense satisfaction of whispering: 'Jenny True.'

Teresa and I were both of us startled.

'Yes,' said Jane. 'He's in love with her, head over ears in love with her.'

Teresa denied it ... she had met Jenny only the other day ... she was sure from what she said...

'Jenny never says,' Jane explained. 'Besides, she may not have realized it yet ... not to the full... I don't believe she does... Jenny's always like that at *the beginning*. Even if she does realize it, she won't admit ... but I'm not judging by that...'

I asked what she was judging by.

Jane said that a month ago Charles was practically engaged to Alice Tiffany, and that now he never went near her. It was all over. For the first time I could see that Teresa began to pay heed to the story. I don't think she was surprised. She had expected something of the sort from the first. Jane said that her daughter Mabel and Alice Tiffany had no secrets from each other, and that Mabel said it was all over. It had happened from the time he met Jenny True at our house. They had met again somewhere in the environs, Jenny had given him a lift. Wilfrid Harris was furious. She knew that for a fact. Whenever Jane said she knew something for a fact, it meant that she thought something, or supposed something. But she was often right. Women have no need of evidence; they have the evidence of their sense.

Then she said: 'Of course, I don't think it matters, and perhaps it will be a good thing for Charles.' She was sorry for Charles, but had no doubt it was all for the best.

I said this explained his absences.

Teresa was indignant, and quite annoyed with Jane. She took up the cudgels for Jenny violently: Jenny was far too sensible to let Charles fall in love with her. She would know how to deal with the situation even if it was true ... perhaps Charles and Alice Tiffany had had a lover's quarrel ... nothing would be more normal ... and as to that, what did the Tiffanys think of their daughter marrying a promising artist with practically no means but his brush?

Jane was fully posted on this.

At first the Tiffanys had been against it, at least Mr Tiffany had been against it. Then he had been impressed by what he had been told by people in Rome, not only artists but a dealer, about the possible market value of Charles' work in the future.

The Tiffanys were not well off. Mr Tiffany had been very well off at one moment, then something had happened in Wall Street, and his fortune had practically all gone ... then he had worked hard, and more or less made good. They had enough to live on, but Mr Tiffany was old now and not well. He had to spend the winter in Europe. He would never be able to work hard again. He would have liked an affluent son-in-law ... however ... she didn't think he would oppose the match, but he would be distinctly relieved if it were to come to nothing.

Teresa went on saying there was nothing in it, and that Jenny was sensible.

'Jenny is sensible,' said Jane with emphasis, 'but in spite of all her experience, she is quite unconscious of her attractiveness at *first* – until it's too late and the mischief is done ... and, as for Charles, he's no idea what Jenny is like.'

Then she told us of what Charles had said to her when she sat next to him at dinner at the Tiffanys. Charles, according to Jane (and no doubt this account was slightly coloured by a subsequent fact or theory), had been silent and absent-minded till she had mentioned the name of Jenny True. Charles had at once then come to life. His face had lit up. Did I know her well? Jane had told him she was an old friend, and Charles had said, reflectively:

'She *is* a jolly woman.'

'I laughed at that,' said Jane; 'it seemed to me such a funny description of Jenny. Charles was quite annoyed at my laughter, and asked if I didn't think she was a jolly woman. I said I did indeed ... I agreed ... but it was not as I would have put it. How would I have put it? I didn't know. I said I thought she was a very charming woman.'

'Yes,' said Charles, 'and good.'

'Good?' I asked.

He said she was beautiful, and all beautiful – really beautiful women were good. Didn't I agree? I was amazed at these words from the lips of Charles. I said I thought it depended on what one called 'beautiful' and what one called 'good'. He said he supposed that everyone must think Mrs True beautiful. I said most people did. I said I thought Alice Tiffany one of the most beautiful girls I had ever seen. Charles said, 'Oh, yes, of course.' Then I said you never saw Jenny before the other day. He said, 'No, never,' and seemed a little bit embarrassed. 'And never since?' I asked. He paused, obviously embarrassed now, but the conversation was interrupted; it became general.

'Of course,' she explained, 'she didn't want to say a word against Jenny ... nobody was fonder of Jenny than she was; but Charles imagined her to be what she had never pretended to be, the embodiment of all the virtues. Jane laughed. 'He imagines her as a kind of saint. I had no idea he was so naive ... no idea, and the funny part is that he isn't – not in all things.'

I was convinced. I thought the story was exaggerated, but that there was something in it.

We changed the subject, and we did not talk of Charles or Jenny any more till Jane had left us.

When she was gone, I said to Teresa that I thought it was a bad business.

'What?' she asked, knowing full well what I meant.

I said: 'About Jenny True and Charles. It

was a mistake their ever meeting.'

Teresa refrained from pointing out that I had been mainly responsible for the occurrence, and that I had brought it about against her wishes and advice; but I did not think of this then. I said it quite sincerely, not dreaming I was to blame.

Teresa merely said that she did not expect that there was anything in it. If Charles was really fond of Alice Tiffany, it would not all come to an end because he had met Jenny once. Jane was a gossip; she always exaggerated and made mountains out of molehills. She was an incurable romantic.

Then I got on my high horse. Possibly there was nothing in it, but whatever there was in it, it must be stopped, and at least *I* was the person to stop it. Charles was too good to waste, and if he was going to spend his whole time with Jenny True and all that gang, he would soon be worn out and quite unfit for any work; he would never paint another picture – that was the important part; his work, not his morals. We were not to forget, I added, that we had a certain degree of responsibility for bringing him to Naples.

Teresa sighed, thinking perhaps and probably of the stupidity of husbands. Again she made no comment, but merely asked:

'How can we stop it?'

I said I would be frank with Charles, explain Jenny's situation to him ... quite kindly and quite nicely, of course, and point out to him how useless it would be for him to look for anything in that quarter, and how he would only make himself ridiculous. I would make him see things as they were ... as he was a reasonable boy, and I thought, trusted and liked me ... he would be sure to listen to reason.

'I shouldn't say anything, Horace,' said Teresa.

'And leave it?' I asked.

Teresa said: 'We could try and distract him.' She would see Jenny, but not mention it to her, of course, but she would soon see how the matter stood. She thought it would be a fatal mistake to say anything – for anyone and most of all for me to say anything to Charles.

I again became eloquent. I assured her she was wrong. Nobody had a greater respect for her judgement than I had, and as I had always told her, I took her advice on anything and everything. She was my best, my only critic – this was true. I thought I took her advice, but I understand now that I seldom did – but in this particular case I did think I was the better judge. I thought this was one of those rare cases when a man's judgement was better than a woman's. I knew Charles, I said, better than she did.

'That's the very reason,' said Teresa, 'why I think it would be a mistake for you to say anything to him. If you so much as hint anything against Jenny, he will not only disbelieve you, but he will hate you.'

I said I would certainly not dream of anything so crude as hinting anything against Jenny.

'Well, then, what?' she asked.

'I have a far better and far subtler plan... I will give him an object-lesson, and easily prove to him that it is not worth his while giving his heart or his thoughts or anything else to Jenny.'

'What object-lesson?' asked Teresa, but at that moment Giovanni, our servant, announced, 'la Signora True.'

Five minutes later Charles walked into the room.

CHAPTER 4

One look at Charles' face when he came into the room that afternoon was enough for Teresa and myself. We saw that Teresa was right.

As for Jenny ... well, there is the difficulty. I am certain that if Jane Sedley had been there, or Countess Zikov, whom nothing escapes, they would have said she was being 'coquette' and perilously so ... but was she? I do not think that at this moment she was giving a thought to Charles. We talked about his pictures ... and I remember asking him to show us something he had done lately... Charles rushed upstairs and brought down some sketches. I noted they had all been done some time ago, only one of them had been done at Naples, and that was before he had been introduced to Jenny.

Jenny looked at the pictures, but limited herself to a swift inspection and to the quickest possible civil appreciation. She was clearly not interested, and did not pretend to be. Landscapes bored her – the kind that

Charles painted – she preferred a more finished style. Charles did not notice it.

Then she asked after the portrait he was doing of Teresa. Could she see it?

'Oh, no, not possibly,' said Charles, 'it is not in a state in which it could be shown.'

The truth was that during the last fortnight he had not asked Teresa to give him a single sitting, on the plea that he wanted to leave it for a while and return to it with a fresh eye.

Again and again Teresa had asked him when the next sitting was to be, and he had always put her off with an excuse. What he said to Jenny was absurd, because he had let me see the portrait, although he had not shown it to Teresa. He never let his sitters see his work until it was finished.

We had both of us been disappointed that he had stopped painting this picture, because I thought it promised to be the finest thing he had done – far finer than his portrait of Mrs H–

Mrs H– was an easier subject, a radiant beauty, but Teresa was a different matter altogether.

Teresa had beauty, and just the kind of beauty that can be painted by a man of genius, and by a man of genius only. She had line and distinction, and a fascinating ivory pallor, and soft, sensible eyes ... eyes that reminded you of Dante's description of Sordello; something slow and serious: 'E nel muover degli occhi onesta e tarda'.

Teresa was just the subject for Charles. But it struck me in a flash while he was talking that he no longer wanted to paint Teresa. He wanted to paint Jenny, and the picture of Teresa would never be finished. My soul was prophetic. I feared Teresa was thinking the same thing.

Jenny was unconscious of this. I felt she had never given a thought to Charles as an artist. She honestly did not care. It was not that she had not taste. She had a natural instinct for beautiful surroundings and pretty objects; but art in the sense in which Charles practised it, and all that it meant to him, was a sealed book to her; besides this, she did not care for his style; she disliked the modern.

Jenny did not stay long that day, but as she left us she said openly to Charles:

'We shall meet tonight.'

In the course of our conversation, Jenny had said that the Tiffanys were leaving Naples, and Charles had added:

'Yes, the climate of Naples doesn't suit Mr Tiffany. It's too cold for him.'

I asked whether they would be coming

back, and Charles said they were going to Egypt and would go straight back from there to Marseilles, and thence to America. He seemed to take it in the most matter-of-fact way.

A day or two later we saw Jane once more, and she was as usual full of news.

Alice Tiffany had told her daughter that it was all over. That there never had been anything. That Charles and she had always been great friends, and had had great fun together, but he had never spoken a serious or an intimate word to her.

Mabel did not believe this was true. At least not as regards Alice. It was possible Charles had never spoken a serious word to her. But Mabel thought he soon would have done so if Jenny had not appeared on the scene. She was convinced the whole matter had come to an end, after that day on which Jenny had given Charles a lift. She said there had been a more or less definite idea of a dinner party on the following Wednesday ... it had been left a little vague, as Alice was not certain at the time whether she would be at Naples, but the arrangement was that it was to happen if she was there.

In the meantime Charles arranged something with Jenny, or, rather, Jenny arranged something with Charles. Charles subsequently said he would come late. The dinner took place, and Charles did come late, but so late that Alice had gone to bed. Mabel was sure this had been a great disappointment to Alice, but the disappointment happened the night we were there, and Alice had said what she said to her mother to shield Charles.

Jane took a serious view of the matter. She said that Jenny was to blame. Teresa still defended her, and still stuck to her point that it was nothing serious. I said nothing. I was brooding on my project.

The days passed. Nothing new or startling happened. Teresa asked me whether I still meant to give Charles an object lesson. I said 'Yes, if it is necessary. I fear it will be necessary. Jenny will lead anyone on if one gives her the vestige of an opening. In two minutes all is up for the man. We must at all costs save Charles. It wouldn't matter if it wasn't for his work. But Jenny would be the ruin of his work ... you see already he is doing nothing. There's that magnificent portrait of you, only half begun, and now it will never be finished. If you don't believe what I've been saying, I will prove it to you.'

Teresa asked how I would prove it.

I said that was my secret. She would see

soon enough.

'I implore you not to interfere,' Teresa said; 'let things take their course. You will only make it worse if you interfere.'

I said I cared far too much for Charles' work and his career not to interfere. It would be sinful not to, as I knew I could interfere successfully.

'But if you make things worse?' she said.

'I shan't make things worse,' I answered; 'there is no chance of that.'

'Well,' said Teresa, 'one never knows, and I think it's always a mistake to interfere with the designs of Providence.'

I said we were the instruments of Providence and had our parts to play. Teresa said we were the actors and should not try and interfere with the author or the stage-manager.

'Besides,' she added, 'sometimes one deceives one's self.'

'There's no danger of that,' I said.

Then suddenly Charles had a bout of serious work. He gave Teresa another sitting, and we thought all was well. We did not know at the time that Jenny had gone to Rome for a week. We never mentioned Jenny to Charles. Jane was laid up with a cold. We saw nobody who belonged to Jenny's world, so we were without news.

One day there came an invitation from Jenny to dine with her. Charles was invited. Teresa wanted us not to go. I insisted.

We went and found the usual gang of people. Jane was there. Charles was in high spirits, but Jenny did not pay more attention to him than to anyone else.

After dinner they were talking of Lady Hamilton, and someone said her villa had been close by at Posilippo; and I told the story, which is to be found in Goethe's *Italienische Reise* and in French memoirs of the time, how after dinner she would take some shawls and imitate the pose of famous statues, so that, as Goethe said, the statues seemed to come to life, although, in fact, as a spiteful French memoirist says, she had little education and no culture. This last point was mentioned and discussed. Someone said it wasn't true, and that it was the French-woman's malice. Upon which Jenny said:

'I daresay it was true; there would be nothing odd about it if it was true. I can prove it to you, because I believe I can do the same thing – not so well, of course – although I have no education and no culture.'

She fetched two shawls. She was dressed in something long, clinging white, classical and soft ... she let down her hair, and in a flash gave us a series of wonderful *tableaux vivants*... She became a goddess, a nymph, a Sibyl, a Muse, a Fury, a Maenad... I had always thought Jenny engaging and graceful and plastic, but I had no idea until that moment what a store of hidden and subtle beauty was at her disposal ... she did what Goethe described Lady Hamilton as doing ... with the same swift changes and unerring truth of expression... She knelt, she stood, she lay down ... she imitated ancient and modern art. At one moment she was as majestic as Proserpine, the next ethereal as Psyche with her perilous lamp, gay as Flora leading on the spring, tragic as Medea, terrible as Medusa, forlorn as Ariadne, desolate as Niobe; and then, changing to modern times, she was as young as Juliet leaning from her balcony, as lovelorn as Guinevere watching for Lancelot, as holy as Joan of Arc.

We were all of us amazed. Her lines, her shoulders, her arms and her neck, and her small head seemed to obey a mysterious rhythm. She seemed to step into the dimension of *time*. She had secret springs of motion, and her changes and her fire, depth, and softness of expression would have been the envy not of a good but of a great actress.

Charles was delirious.

'I will paint her as Joan of Arc,' he said. 'That was the best of all. That is whom she is really like.'

I asked Jenny afterwards, when we were having supper, whether she had had any training ... whether she had ever acted.

She said that her father used to make her act when she was a little girl, and teach her how to move. He had been a great lover of the ballet in his day. Her mother, too, had a passion for the stage, but she hadn't encouraged it in her daughter; she was afraid of her going on the stage. In Paris she had lessons in elocution from a woman who had been a famous actress at the Comédie Française, Madame Blançon. She had had dancing lessons, too, from a man who had once been ballet master at Moscow, but had had to leave Russia owing to his political opinions.

'So you see,' she said, smiling, 'I have been very well taught.'

'Didn't they want you to go on the stage?' I asked.

'Madame Blançon did,' she said, 'but she wanted me to go on to the French stage ... and I did think of it when my father died, but I think it would have killed my mother, and, besides that, I didn't think my French was good enough. It was good, but not good enough. And then, when I was thinking of the English stage, I got engaged to be married.'

'And that, as usual, was the end of art,' said Jane, 'as it always is. The two are incompatible. If you serve Art, you must serve her and her only. She is a jealous goddess. It's a pity, because you would have been a great actress.'

'I don't think I could have done the words,' said Jenny, 'and then, I was too nervous whenever I was on the stage.'

'Oh, nonsense,' said Teresa, 'do you remember that day you recited a scene from *Andromaque* at Madame Dellion's? You made a sensation.'

'Yes,' said Jenny, 'but I suffered a great deal too much.'

As we were driving home, I said to Teresa: 'You never told me Jenny could act.'

She said she had forgotten all about it. It appears that Jenny used constantly to recite both in French and in German, and that Madame Blançon used to say she could do anything with her. She was against the English stage, though. She thought it a waste for Jenny, and she did not understand English.

'But she was right about her mother,' she added; 'it would have killed her.'

Charles said nothing all the time we were driving home, but he kept on murmuring to himself some lines of French verse:

Accours, jeune Chromis, je t'aime, et je suis belle,
Blanche comme Diane et légère comme elle!
Comme elle grande et fière; et les bergers, le soir,
Quand le regard baissé, je passe sans les voir,
Doutent si je ne suis qu'une simple mortelle,
Et, me suivant des yeux, disent: 'Comme elle est belle!'

CHAPTER 5

The next day Charles was to have given Teresa a sitting, but just as she was getting ready to go up to his studio, Giovanni brought a message to say he had gone. He had left a hurried note saying he had been obliged to go to Castellamare for two days. He had promised to do a sketch there. Why? And for whom? The note was vague and incoherent.

Jane supplied the explanation. Jenny had gone to Castellamare to stay with her aunt;

she was to be away three days.

When Charles came back, he no longer made any pretence of wanting to go on with regular work. He said he was entirely dissatisfied with his portrait of Teresa, and that he had quite decided to abandon it for a time.

Later on he mentioned casually that he was painting Jenny. He wanted to paint her as Joan of Arc, but she had refused. So he was painting her as Ariadne (just the head and shoulders), lying down with her head resting on an arm against a background of sea – one of the poses she had so beautifully adopted on that memorable evening.

This meant he went to Jenny's villa every day. When I said something about this to Teresa, she said:

'Leave things alone ... at any rate, it has not stopped his painting.'

We both of us recognized the fact that Charles was wildly in love with Jenny, and we thought, from his spirits, his attitude and his general mode of behaviour, that he had perhaps obtained his heart's desire.

Then a curious thing happened. When the picture was finished, after some half-dozen hectic sittings, Jenny was shown it and said she couldn't bear it. She wanted to be painted as she was in her ordinary clothes.

Charles took me to see the picture, and I admitted that Jenny was more than right.

The picture was a disappointment. It was cleverly painted, of course, and extremely well drawn, but all Charles' force and originality seemed to have deserted him. It was a sentimental picture, in the style which, of all others, was most alien to his nature. It was like a bad Leighton, a bad Tadema. It looked as if he had done it for a joke.

He asked me what I thought about it; I was guarded, praised the drapery and the glimpse of Neapolitan sea Charles saw at once that I did not like it.

Then I saw Jenny for a moment alone.

'Isn't it terrible,' she said. 'I admit I am not an artist, and that I don't understand modern painting, and, least of all, Mr Donne's ... but I know and see that what he used to do was clever ... but this is like a chocolate-box, and it's not the least like me. Do beg him to paint me as I am.'

I agreed with Jenny.

She took the line with him of saying she couldn't bear fancy-dress. And, indeed, the whole point of Jenny's tableaux was their motion.

You could not immobilize those poses. Nor could she crystallize the fleeting expression with which she accompanied them.

Charles had tried to do the impossible, and he had not achieved it.

Two days later I asked him about the picture, and he said:

'I have painted it out. I am doing a sketch portrait of her now in a Paris hat. That's what she seems to prefer. I shall finish it in two or three sittings.'

But he never finished it.

Charles never mentioned this new picture, and I heard nothing about it till one day I got a note from Jenny asking me to call that afternoon.

She had evidently chosen the first day when Charles could not be there, as his father had arrived in Rome on his way back from Egypt, and wished to see him. He had left by the night train the night before.

I found Jenny sitting in her garden. It was a lovely day. The sun was hot and the sky clear and open, a sky such as tempts one to adventure. There was a pleasant tramontana blowing.

'I am so glad you have come,' she said. 'I want to speak to you about Mr Donne's picture.'

I asked whether it was finished, and what she thought about it.

'You shall see for yourself,' she said.

She led me into a large empty room on the ground door looking out on to the sea that Charles had used as a studio. The picture (a small canvas) giving just the head, stood on an easel.

Jenny pointed to it without a word.

It had the same defects as the other, only it was worse. It was difficult to believe it was Charles' work. It was sentimental; a caricature of Jenny. It missed everything in her that was personal and individual, and it looked like a fashion plate.

I said nothing. There was nothing to say. She understood my silence.

I asked her what he thought of it himself.

'He knows it's dreadful,' she said, 'but he says it's all my fault for not letting him paint me as Joan of Arc. That's what he wanted to do, and it's too absurd.' She laughed.

'What are we to do?' I asked.

'Nothing,' she said. 'There's nothing to be done, except for him not to paint me at all ... you see, frankly, Mr St Clair, I can't bear his pictures, none of them. I like Mr Donne enormously, but I can't bear his pictures, and I do think that these are worse than the others ... and is that like me?'

I said it was worse than the others and

certainly not in the least like her.

She gave a sigh of relief.

'Well, you think I'm right not to let him try something else?'

'Quite right,' I said.

'And Joan of Arc least of all.'

I said I didn't think he could do it, beautiful as the impersonation had been.

Then we went out into the garden and talked of other things. She talked of Charles in an easy, detached way. He was a child, such a baby in some ways...

I told her she was distracting him from his work.

'His work!' she said. 'He has been doing nothing but work, painting me all these weeks.'

'That's just it,' I said.

Then I flattered her. I said what I thought was true, that nobody could paint her, least of all Charles, and that it was insane to try and catch those gleams of genius she had given us the other night.

'That's all nonsense,' she said, 'I don't give these things a thought ... it was only a joke ... anyone could do it who has the ghost of a figure, and I have always been taught to sit up and walk straight, and all that kind of thing. I had a severe governess, and father was particular, too. He couldn't bear anything slipshod, and my mother had a natural knack and flair for walking, clothes, dancing, and all that sort of thing.'

I told her that I thought her poses quite unforgettable. I became eloquent. I begged to be allowed to come and see them again. I said she had no idea how good they were. It was she who was the great artist, not Charles. She was an artist in life.

She listened civilly without seeming to pay much attention, and when once I ventured on a rather excessive compliment, veiling it carefully, she looked at me and smiled and said:

'Don't *you* pay that kind of compliment. It's not worthy of you.'

We had tea on the terrace. I gave up compliments. We talked of all sorts of things. Of her youth, of Paris, of her early aspirations, of the people at Naples, of the Tiffanys.

I said I had thought at one time that Charles had been in love with Alice.

'It would have done very well,' she said. 'I think he could have painted *her*.'

'He could have painted her mother,' I said. 'Miss Tiffany is beautiful, but she has no expression.'

Then Captain Harris arrived, and I left. I

71

asked, when I was going, if I might come again. She said: 'Yes, any day you like. I am always here, I seldom go out to things ... I am lazy.'

'May I come tomorrow?' I asked.

She seemed not at all surprised, but thought a moment, and then said:

'Yes, tomorrow, of course. Come to luncheon and bring Teresa. I think Mr Donne's got his father here for two days. You will meet some rather nice people.'

I left her.

The next day I asked Teresa to plead a headache and let me go to Jenny's alone. I said I had begun my scheme.

Teresa assented at once, but begged me not to go on with my scheme, whatever it was.

'No good will come of it,' she said.

But I was obstinate. I thought I knew better.

I went and found only a few Italians, regular guests. After luncheon I stayed on and had another talk with Jenny. I found her society enchanting, and while I was with her I could easily imagine myself to be in love with her, but directly I left her I did not give her a thought – at least that is what I said to myself at the time.

We got to know each other well in a short space of time. Charles was to be away a week. One morning I took her to the Museum. One night she dined with us. I saw her almost every day, but seldom alone.

The night before Charles was coming back, Teresa said to me:

'Do take care, it will all end so badly.'

Then a telegram came from Charles, saying that his father was laid up. And later another telegram that he was obliged to take his father to England.

I went to see Jenny to tell her the news. I found her alone. She knew about Charles already.

'I suppose you hear from him every day?' I asked.

'Sometimes twice a day,' she said, laughing, 'not counting the telegrams.'

'It was very wicked of you,' I said, 'to trifle with a boy like that.'

'I didn't encourage him,' she said, 'and you must admit that. He will get over it at once. When he comes back from England, if he does come back, he will have quite forgotten me. You see, artists are never in love with anyone for long. They can't be. They are in love with their art, and they must have change. Charles was in love with

Alice Tiffany, just for a short time. He admitted it to me himself, at least, he said he would have been in love with her if he hadn't met me, and I know that is true. He never proposed to her, or, indeed, said anything like that. I never meant to take him away from Alice. I never gave it a thought. I never somehow thought a young artist like that would be fond of me. He was so unlike anyone I had ever met before.'

I told her she must have known perfectly well.

'You must know that you have charm and beauty.'

'I never thought he would or could be fond of me,' she said. 'That is the truth.'

I was about to declare myself, when we were interrupted by callers. I arranged to see her the next day, but when the next day came I got a telegram from her asking me not to come, as she was not well.

I went to enquire and left her some flowers. They told me at the door that the signora was indisposed with a terrible headache. The weather had been bad and there was a sirocco. I went the next day, and again I was not allowed in.

Then I wrote her a long letter. I told her what I imagine she had been told by countless others, what she was being told by countless others, over and over again, every day: I said she had changed my existence; that I had never known what real love was before; that she had never met with love of that kind, that I loved her differently; for her *real* self; that I couldn't live without her; that she had turned my life, my soul and my heart inside out. That I could neither eat, sleep nor work... I was eloquent ... and not literary ... the letter was badly written, and honestly badly written ... not badly written on purpose... I said to myself that I almost believed what I was writing while I wrote it... Jenny, so I said, had become translated for me into the realm of fiction ... and then I have, when I don't try, a certain convincing gift of expression ... when I try, I *please,* but I don't convince ... hence the great success of the *Silver Pound.* I was not trying... I think my letter must have had a ring of reality... I didn't read it through... It was full of blots, written with oh! such a pen, with feelers like a sea beast ... on such paper too ... it was long.

Only in writing this letter and in sending her this letter, please, please, remember this; please, please understand this; I never for one moment expected Jenny to take it seriously: I expected her to read it, tear it up, relegate it to the file of her amatory experiences and smile ... to take it at its real value ... and to approve... My idea of Jenny at this epoch was this: or rather what I said to myself was this:

I am playing an opening, as well-known as the Ruy Lopez or the Knight's gambit opening in chess, or leading the fourth best at whist, in a game in which she is a professional. A game which she is not willing to play except with people of her own recognized ability in that game ... her own 'class' in the modern sense of the word ... that is to say, a chosen few ... who not only play the same rules as she does ... but who are in her 'class', up to her 'form'. She knows and practises the same conventions ... gives and demands the same attention, the same skill and the same knowledge ... not only that; she abides by the same imponderable standard; the same unwritten laws; she observes the same ritual... I said I have only to make the first initial move and she will instantly answer the opening. The game will proceed. And the result will be that Charles will lose, and, by losing, win.

I said to myself: 'I am doing this for Charles; I will prove to him exactly what kind of woman Jenny is, and, when he realizes that he has been shelved for me just because I happen to be older, better known, established, and surrounded by the glamour of notoriety, while he is still only a promising artist known to a restricted circle of artists and a few buyers, he will understand; even if he is annoyed at first, he will ultimately understand and, in the end, be grateful to me.'

I thought that Jenny was already bored with Charles. Whatever Jenny might say now, I was convinced that she had behaved deliberately. That she must have known perfectly well that but for her Charles would have proposed to Alice Tiffany, who, after all, would have made an admirable wife for him.

I am still of that opinion, after all those years. I still think that he would not only have been happy had he married Alice Tiffany, but that it would have been the solution of his life – but how his art would have fared is another matter. Jenny said she had done nothing to lead him on. I know now in a sense that this was true: I thought she had just used her fine technique and set going the well-oiled wheels of a delicate piece of machinery. I now know I was wrong. It was far more subtle than that. Jenny had never really given a thought either to Charles or to Alice Tiffany.

The experienced reader will snort and will say every woman knows that kind of thing at once, and Jenny True was not only an experienced woman of the world, but highly intuitive; a woman of great experience in the affairs of the heart; an expert on the hearts of men.

The truth is hardly ever believed, but how far more interesting it is – not than fiction but than convention. Jenny was too busy to give a thought to Charles. She didn't care for him. She was not interested in him. She did not much care for artists, and she happened to dislike, not only then, but always, his particular form of art. If she were alive now, she'd still detest his pictures. They were not the style of thing she either understood or liked.

She had a definite taste of her own. She may not have been artistic, but she was fastidious in all things, according to her own standards; she was extremely independent; she knew exactly what she liked, and was not ashamed of it. Her standards were curious; they were, for her time, old-fashioned; they would have been old-fashioned in any epoch. But then the experienced reader will say:

'If she didn't care, why didn't she prevent it?'

She didn't prevent it because it happened before she realized it. Charles was infected with the microbe in a flash, just at the critical moment of his relations with Alice Tiffany. After that it was too late.

Jenny could no more have prevented this than she could prevent being herself. It had been enough for Charles to see her once and to be given a lift, in a carriage. Jenny could not help being all that was most calculated to attract Charles.

But then it will be argued: 'She needn't have gone any further. She might have said: "I'm not that kind of woman, and goodbye."'

But that was unlike Jenny. Her whole point was that she never said: 'I am not that kind of woman.' She would have said, 'I *am* that kind of woman, but I don't happen to be fond of you, not in that way ... or else I am fond of you, and if you feel like that and I am making you unhappy, then why not? I don't think these things matter.'

She liked Charles. She liked his looks, his personality. She liked his admiration. Jenny could not resist admiration and appreciation. Can anyone? Yes, from those they dislike; but from those they like? He was something new and fresh to her, but she never realized his nature ... not at that moment at least ... nor what she was doing to him, because she did not really care for him. She was not in love with him, either then or ever. I knew that. My point was that there were so many other flies in her web. There was Wilfrid Harris, Adderly, a Frenchman, at least two Italians I knew, and probably others I knew nothing of. Why should she annex Charles when she did not care for him and when it might play such havoc in his life and in his work?

I thought to myself: 'I will supplant him and show him how little she cares: that what she likes is the glamour of achievement, and that youth has no chance against maturity and experience, an established name and a European notoriety... It will sicken him of her, and he will see things as they are, and Jenny as she really is, and all will be well.'

The moral of it all was that it is easy to be wise after the event, and that Teresa was right when she said it was a mistake to meddle with the plans of Providence. But the fact is that at the time I thought I was playing an amazingly successful game in the saving of Charles' artistic soul from the fire.

I see now my fatuity and my ignorance, my blindness and my folly, as clearly as any human being has ever seen anything, although I was old enough and experienced enough to know better then. Even then, had I been dealing with such a subject in a book, I should have gauged the situation accurately; even then, if a friend had told me of a fictitious or real case of the kind, and had asked my opinion, I should probably have given admirable advice, right advice; but as I was myself in question, in spite of all Teresa's warnings and hints, I was blind and deaf. There was a mist before my eyes, which only lifted when it was too late.

CHAPTER 6

Jenny answered my letter. She said she was well again. My letter had surprised her. She had valued my friendship and hoped to go on doing so, if I would be sensible; but her life was too full already and too complicated to admit of any new intimate relation ... any new friendship. She hoped to see me later ... but she would rather I did not come at present. She could not explain... It made things difficult for her and she was sure I would understand.

81

I said to myself the letter was perhaps another correct move in a classical opening, and that my correct counter-move would be to take no notice but to go and see her at once.

I did, and I was told that the Signora had left Naples. She had gone to Castellamare. They had no idea when she was coming back.

I was not only annoyed, but really disappointed. I worked myself up into a fever of irritation, of impatience and resentment. I imagined that I cared far more than I did: that is what I said to myself, then.

A few days passed. We heard from Charles, from the country, in England. He had got his father home with difficulty, and he was still far from well. The doctor, however, hoped now that he was at home he would pull through. It was impossible, Charles said, for him to leave his father at present. He was still in a critical condition.

I called every day at Jenny's villa and never obtained anything but the vaguest news. She might come back soon, or she might not.

Then one of the English residents, a Mrs Carthew, who had a beautiful villa, asked us to dinner. She was half Italian and lived in the Bohemian world. She had married an

English novelist who was much younger than herself. He wrote successful and popular novels of a straightforward kind, full of simple love-interest, and loaded with local colour.

Teresa said to me, 'Shall we go?'

I said I felt disinclined to dine out...Teresa said, 'We shall have to go some time, or they will think you are being superior. Carthew is so touching in his genuine admiration for your work.'

So we went, and the first person I saw when we came into the room was Jenny.

I went up to her as soon as I could. I thought she looked a little tired. She was standing away from the other guests. I said to her in a low voice:

'I'm so glad to see you before we go.'

'Are you going?' she said.

'Yes,' I said, 'we are going back to Rome. We are tired of Naples.'

I had invented this plan on the spur of the moment. Until that moment I had no idea of leaving Naples ... but I was prepared to make it true... At any rate I thought it was the right move... But as I said it Jenny's face changed ... over her face there passed one of those swift changes of expression which were so marvellous when she posed for us...

A swift look of profound disappointment, followed by an expression of pain – real pain – as if someone had stabbed her with something sharp. She recovered herself instantly.

I said to myself, 'Now, is that acting or not? She could do it – that we know – when she did Ariadne it was like that' ... and yet I thought it was not acting... Again, I said to myself, 'that is probably your own conceit... She is fooling you ... there is no limit to the deceit and artifices of women, or to the stupidity of men...'

We went in to dinner. I did not sit next to, but opposite, her. She seemed absent-minded at dinner. She repeated what her neighbours said to her, just echoing their phrases, and I felt her mind was far away ... or was that too the perfection of acting?... And whenever I said anything, she listened, laughed, and joined in the conversation across the table when it was possible. We all got up together; the men went into a smoking-room and stayed a long time, and nobody joined us.

Among them was l'Abbé X–, who lived in Rome, and was well-known for his classical and archaeological erudition. I had met him often in Rome and knew him well. He was an oldish man with very clear, birdlike eyes and a charming smile that had nothing seminarist or even clerical about it ... it was the smile of kindness and goodwill.

We had a long talk after dinner. He had read my books. He was interested in psychology, and questions of conscience, and the rendering of them in fiction, and I often used to consult him. He preferred my serious work, and he said to me, 'As for your *Rouge Liard*, whatever it is called ... *je ne crois pas que cela soit de vous.*'

I asked him laughingly whom he thought it was by.

'*Nous avons tous un petit lutin,*' he said, '*qui nous souffle de temps en temps des folies dour nous distraire – des folies charmantes – du reste.*'

While I was talking to him I was thinking the whole time of Jenny. What was she really thinking and feeling? Supposing she really cared ... would it not perhaps be better to withdraw from the game altogether...? But it was absurd to think she cared ... she couldn't care ... it was her well-known technique, and I was being taken in... I was justified in what I had undertaken. It was more than ever necessary now to save Charles.

I had no chance of talking to Jenny afterwards till just as we were going away, when we found ourselves face to face in a small passage. Teresa had gone to fetch her cloak.

'Are you really going away?' she said.

I nodded.

'Teresa said nothing about it.'

'Teresa doesn't know.'

'But why?' she asked gently.

'Because you are so cruel to me.'

'Oh, Horace...!'

If that was acting, it would have deceived the elect. 'Very well,' I said, 'I won't go.'

Her face lit up. She was transfigured.

She became Flora leading on the spring for the moment.

Teresa called me.

I said good night, and hurried away, but in saying good night Jenny pressed my hand slightly, and I almost thought there was something agonizing, either real or pretended, in that pressure.

I said to myself there seemed to be every hope of saving Charles.

The next day two unexpected things happened. We received a telegram from Charles saying that his father was dead, and that he was coming back as soon as he could; and Teresa got a telegram from her sister who had married a diplomat. They were on their way to Cairo *en poste* and would be stopping a few days in Rome. She begged Teresa to come and see her if she possibly could. Teresa had not seen her for several years, as their last post had been Tokyo.

Teresa consulted me. I at once offered to go to Rome with her. I wanted to go. I thought it would possibly be the right solution – the providential solution.

It was strange how the fictitious plan which I had invented for Jenny's benefit in the game had entered into the region of possibility.

But Teresa would not hear of it.

'Charles,' she said, 'may arrive any minute, and he must find someone here.'

Ultimately it was settled that she should leave that night. We did not settle how long she would stay away.

Before she left, Teresa said to me: 'Do take care, Horace.'

I asked, 'What of?'

'Yourself,' she said.

I said I didn't understand; but she refused to be more explicit: all she said was:

'It's so easy to throw dust in one's own eyes.'

'I won't do that,' I said.

Then I got a note from Jenny saying she could not see me that day, but she asked me to come the day after, any time after three.

I was perplexed.

I went to the Museum in the afternoon, and there I met the Abbé. We looked at many things together, and he was most illuminating in his comments. He asked me to go back to his rooms and have a cup of tea or coffee. I did. He lived on the top floor of a small hotel.

He must have noticed how absent-minded I was, as I found it difficult to play up to his animated conversation. Finally he could bear it no longer, and asked me if I had anything on my mind that was worrying me. I said I had. It was nothing to do with myself personally, but it was a hard case. A *cas de conscience*. I would tell him if he allowed me to do so in terms of *A* and *B*. It concerned friends of mine, friends that he did not know.

He said he would be delighted to listen.

We had on former occasions often discussed similar cases. I told him the story from the point of view of a friend whom I called *A*. I called Charles, *B*, and Jenny, *C*. I told him my scheme and that it was not a thing in the past but was now happening.

There was still time, so I thought then, to withdraw from the game altogether.

The *A* and *B* were only a convention which the Abbé saw through immediately.

He knew that I knew he had seen through it, but we both kept up the convention, more or less. Sometimes the Abbé forgot it and addressed me.

I told him about Charles' achievement, the opinion I had that was shared by others of his powers, what they had thought about him in Paris. The Abbé had never met Charles.

I said I was quite certain that *A*, my friend who was himself an artist, did not care two straws about Charles' morals. On the contrary ... he thought a liaison *of* that kind might be sometimes fruitful, but in this case he dreaded the effect it would have, the effect it had already had on his work.

The Abbé listened intently to the whole story.

He said it was a *sentiment louable*, etc ... on the part of my friend, the wish to help, but he was making *fausse route*. He was afraid he was '*dans une bien mauvaise voie*'. It was measuring things by the wrong standard. It was impossible to measure life by the standard of art without morals ... if you left out *le péché*, in a question of this kind, you left out everything ... he was speaking not only as a priest, but as an ethical doctor – *un vieux médecin qui passe sa vie à apprendre ... à prendre des notes ... à observer cette pauvre*

89

humanité dont on dit tant de mal. Elle est si bonne quand on la voit de près ... a doctor who had experienced the causes and the results of most diseases and disasters: what he was saying was not a matter of theory but a matter of experience and of fact; a matter of common sense. He then apologized a thousand times for saying what he was going to say to a novelist who was famous for his psychology – famous for the truth and insight of his work, which no one admired more than he did.

I felt ashamed of myself when he said this. What after all did my psychology consist of? Blundering guess work, or crumbs from the wisdom of Teresa; and was not my most, my *only* successful work, a fluke?

After the Abbé had finished his preface of delicate compliments, he said:

'I do not think either your friend or yourself fully understand a woman's heart. I do not think your friend realizes that if he is capable of pleasing at all, (and I suppose he must at least think he is capable of playing this comedy *well*, or he would not attempt it at all), that the woman may take the game seriously, and love him *pour de bon*. You cannot say you have a complete knowledge of the other person concerned (*l'autre*) – of

90

the woman. Perhaps she had always been searching for something solid and now thinks, "Well now I have found it at last."

'You know,' he said, 'how sudden are the movements of a woman's heart ... how disguised its sentiments always are, how secret its aspirations. Surely then, your friend ... if he is an artist, with high ideals ... and I assume, if he is a friend of yours whom you esteem, that he is an artist with a high standard and a lofty view ... would fear to touch this mysterious recess (*repli*) with a sacrilegious hand, lest unforeseen things: violations, awakenings, and growths (*poussées*) come about: and births and deaths.'

I said I didn't think there was any danger of that. I knew the woman too well.

'Let us admit that you know her *à fond.*' said the Abbé. 'Have you taken into account what *une vanité froissée* means, and what it may bring forth? Up to the present moment she has been indifferent: she has thought, "Here is another, like the others": is it not possible that she may arm herself against your friend, and capture the other man for good; because she sees that he cares for him more than he cares for her? I do not believe she could tolerate this game, which would signify that she is a woman from whom the other must be "saved" and that your friend means to "save" him.'

I said she wasn't as complicated as all that; she was a light woman.

'*Les femmes les plus légères ont leurs abîmes,*' he said. 'How do you know she is all light? But let us leave her out for a moment, and think for a moment of that excellent young man whom you wish, whom your friend, I mean, wishes to save by this sombre *comédie*. If he loves her, as you say, and she casts him off *now*, he will suffer ... the anguish of youth, fierce, but let us hope, fleeting: we may hope so. But if you force her, as I believe to be possible, to set about capturing him seriously, to keep him an indefinite time and then to *lâcher* him, he will never recover from the rupture when it happens. She will remain in his blood and in his flesh. Or if *le Bon Dieu* wills that he should recover, he will have been so tortured by you that your fine friendship with him will suffer shipwreck for ever in a dark *rancune* ... and he will never forgive you, even when he is cured.'

'He is an artist,' I said, 'he will recover.'

The Abbé said, '*Mon enfant*, do not be cynical; you are lessening and impoverishing the notion of friendship. A true friend who would be loyal through the grief that he

92

is bound to suffer when she drops him, would help to cure him, and lead him to better things.'

I felt the Abbé was right, but I did not drop the cynical note.

'Monsieur l'Abbé,' I said, 'it's his *work* we care for ... we want to get him out of that web; she may not drop him at all; she may keep him indefinitely in the web, where there are all too many flies already, and in the meantime his finest period of productivity will slip by.'

Up to now the Abbé had called me either *cher ami* or *cher enfant*. Now he was annoyed.

'*Mais Monsieur,*' he said, '*c'est une chose abominable que vous faites là.* I say *you*, because if you advise your friend to do this act the fault will be yours as well. You are arrogating to yourself the right of releasing forces that the *Bon Dieu* has placed in the human heart and that only He has the right to manipulate. Give up this folly. It is the folly of an artist who thinks of nothing but the *situation*, the *combinazione*, *la scène à faire* ... *gardez tout cela pour le roman, pour la scène* ... *life* is stronger than you. *Méfiez vous.* All that will recoil on yourself. You will see blood flow and have nothing to bind the mortal wounds with.'

I said that of course if he took that line there was no more to be said ... but I wondered, if he knew the woman and knew the man, whether he would not think differently. After all I didn't care. It wasn't really any business of mine.

'*Mon cher enfant,*' he said, 'you care very much and it does you credit. It's all to the good. Let me appeal to you to show *le vrai esprit de sport* ... which your race, with its frankness and straightness, understands so well. There cannot be here any question of a game, of a comedy. It is a question of souls created and preserved by God for God. You understand so much. Try to see *ce que c'est qu'une âme.*'

'We are talking different languages,' I said. 'Souls in that sense are beyond my horizon.'

I asked him if he had never read Dumas' play – *Le Demi-Monde*, in which the hero saves the young man from marrying an adventuress by making up to her himself.

'Oh! *mon enfant! une pièce!*' said the Abbé, shrugging his shoulders, 'and I understand in your case the woman is not an adventuress, and there is no question of marriage.'

I said she was not an adventuress, and I did not think she would ever contemplate marrying the young man, although I had no doubt he would want to marry her...

'There,' said the Abbé, 'is the danger of literature, the *snare* of literature, and you know nobody loves letters more than I do; but you men of letters always get back to art instead of to life; you think of things in situations ... but I have said that before.'

'I think you are right,' I said. 'I will try and do better.'

The Abbé laughed. I left him presently. As I went away he said:

'Beg your friend to think things over and to do nothing hastily, and give him good advice.'

CHAPTER 7

I thought the Abbé was right, but then (I thought) he did not know Jenny. He had only met her casually. Here I was mistaken. He knew Jenny and he had known her mother. Nor did he, I said, know Charles. I took Teresa to the station. She promised to write every day. I told her that if her sister was staying any time in Rome, and she wanted me to join her, I would come at a moment's notice.

The next afternoon I went to see Jenny. I found her in a different mood from the night of the dinner. Calm, self-possessed, serene ... and gay. We sat on the terrace.

'I have been thinking things over,' she said, 'and I am now clothed and in my right mind. I haven't been well lately, but now I have recovered. You must forget anything I have said up to now. There is no reason we shouldn't be friends, and good friends ... no reason you shouldn't come and see me in reason ... only I insist on one or two conditions.'

I asked what they were.

She said they could all of them be summed up in one condition: 'No more nonsense.'

'Do not let us have any more make-believe,' she said. 'You don't care for me, and I know you don't; so why pretend? It's not worthy of you. Why go through all the forms of a rather tiresome comedy that means nothing and simply makes things difficult?

'Even if you did care it would be a pity, because I could give you nothing ... my life is full... But the main point is, you don't care ... you are fond of Teresa ... you have your work ... your life is full; and besides, Teresa is an old friend of mine and I am very fond of her ... so it would be wrong and silly from every point of view.'

'But supposing I *do* care?' I said.

'Then in that case,' she said, gently but quite firmly, 'it's goodbye ... I mean it ... I really mean it ... only if you promise to forget all that ... all that nonsense ... it needn't be goodbye.'

I said I would accept her conditions. She talked of other things, and I had not been there long before she said she wanted to introduce me to a charming Italian friend of hers who was coming in a moment.

The Italian friend, Countess R–, arrived. I stayed a moment. More people arrived, and I left her. As I was going she said, 'If you care to dine here tonight, you will find friends.'

I accepted.

I went for a walk in the town and strolled into a café. There to my astonishment I met an old friend of mine I had not seen for years: Godfrey Law. He was my contemporary, we had learnt German together at Heidelberg, and had known each other later in London and Paris. He had then gone into the Diplomatic Service. He had done well. He was now on the verge of being a Minister.

I had never known anyone so intimately as I knew Godfrey, but I had not seen him for many years. He seemed delighted to see me, and not, I thought, at all altered ... his hair was grey at the temples but still thick ... he looked a little tighter, a little more pinched; but he had the same vivacity and the same natural elegance; the same complete absence of pompousness which made him successful and rare as a diplomat.

He explained that he was on his way back to London from Cairo. He had exchanged with someone in the Foreign Office for six months. He hoped then to get a good post as First Secretary or Minister.

He had passed through Rome, and as he was in Rome he thought he might just as well visit Naples, which he had never seen.

This struck me as a little bit odd and improbable. The Godfrey Law I had known never did anything without some sound reason. Just to see Naples seemed hardly enough. I asked him if he was staying long, and whether he was alone.

'I'm only staying a day and a night,' he said. 'I just wanted a glimpse of the place. If one doesn't snatch these opportunities when they come, they never come again.'

I asked him whether he knew anyone at Naples.

'Only one person,' he said – 'Jenny True. I

am dining with her tonight.'

'I know her too, and am dining there too – so you know her?'

'I used to know her,' he said, 'very well.'

I felt a pang of jealousy, doubt and suspicion. Had Godfrey been one of her lovers? Was that the reason he was at Naples? Nothing would be more probable.

I remembered a host of incidents ... how easily triumphant he used to be in all social matters ... how one felt like a pedant or a pedagogue or an oaf, a boor or a bore directly he came into the room ... he was so easy ... so natural ... he turned water into something sparkling with bubbles in it...

I tried then to stifle my pang of jealousy ... which was really social jealousy, not love-jealousy; jealousy caused by my sense of social inadequacy, inferiority in the art of living, and not jealousy on account of Jenny...

Then he said: 'I have known Jenny ever since she was a girl. I knew her before she was out ... she was the most charming girl you ever saw... I knew her father, too ... he was charming; a genius in his way ... and her mother ... poor thing! She was so pretty and so kind! Then I saw Jenny when she was engaged; she asked me if I thought it was a mistake... I said yes, heartily. She said she was afraid it was, but she meant to do it. Then I said, of course, there was nothing more to be said, and there wasn't. After that I didn't see her for some time. I knew Sir J–. I rather liked him. I got on with him. He was extraordinarily clever.'

'Was she very much in love with him?' I asked.

'No, not a bit ... it just happened ... she was wonderfully good to him.'

'But I suppose not very faithful?'

'Oh!' said Godfrey, 'Jenny can't help just taking anyone she sees ... it's second nature to her... This is what happens... She sees someone ... they are of course attracted ... she takes no notice ... *honestly* no notice ... then they catch fire, then she says, "Let's stop all this nonsense and be friends!" If they take her at her word she lets things be, despising them, laughing at them – saying, not openly, but to herself – *"imbécile"*, and if they don't; if they persist and become violent, she gives in ... and then it lasts a short or a long time, as things may be, and she forgets all about it. I have seen it happen over and over again ... but I have never known her care desperately, care really for anyone yet, except for that young idiot she married. She certainly adored him.'

'Doesn't she care for Wilfrid Harris?' I asked, rather unsteadily.

All jealousy of Godfrey had melted now in a feeling of bitter rage against Jenny and bitter contempt for myself. Godfrey had so exactly described her technique with regard to me.

'I believe he is the *maître en titre,*' he said, 'but there are others; young Alfredo Gallazzi is wildly in love with her ... and I expect several others.'

I felt, as Godfrey told me all this, that it never occurred to him for a moment that there was a possibility of my knowing Jenny well. He evidently ruled that out of court, and it slightly humiliated me.

He talked about Teresa. He had seen her in Rome. He told me, what I knew already, that she was staying on a few days, and I made up my mind then and there that I would join her at once; but I meant first to have it out with Jenny ... to show her I was not quite such a fool as she thought.

I walked back with Godfrey to his hotel. We met at Jenny's in the evening.

Godfrey sat next to Countess Zikov, whom I had met there before. I was between a stranger and Jane Sedley. Jane knew Godfrey well, too, and I asked her why he had come to Naples.

The reason, she said – in her usual confidential tone – was his neighbour, Countess Zikov. They had been in love with each other for years, but they seldom met. Vera's husband was jealous, and Godfrey moved from post to post, but they managed to meet sometimes at out-of-way places, such as Naples, Paris or St Moritz. Zikov was at present at Rome at the Embassy.

'They had probably planned this months ago,' said Jane.

'Then Godfrey was never in love with Jenny,' I said.

'Oh, never! they were friends in youth; children together, almost like brother and sister. And you know why Godfrey is going to London?'

I said I had no idea.

'It's because they say Zikov will probably be appointed to the Embassy there, as Second Secretary, or something. Nobody knows that yet, and it's not settled, but Jenny told me.'

I had no opportunity of talking to Jenny alone that night. She seemed happy and gay, and she was looking her best. We made her do some of her 'poses' after dinner. Godfrey stage-managed them and made her do new ones we had never seen: notably a lovely one of the 'Sleeping Beauty'.

She was bewitching.

I left late. Godfrey said he was staying on another night. Jane said that Countess Zikov was going back to Rome the next evening. Godfrey was evidently staying to see the last of her. He was leaving for London the next day.

I asked him to dine with me alone on the following evening, and he accepted.

That afternoon I went to see Jenny. I found her alone. She seemed a little surprised to see me, a little surprised altogether. I think she sensed there was something in the air.

I had settled now once and for all that Charles must be saved by any means whatsoever; whatever the Abbé might say. He had been wrong, and I had been right about Jenny.

'I didn't expect you today,' she said, 'and you can't stay long because I am just going out. I have ordered the carriage. I have got a great many things to do. I asked you to come within reason, but I can't see you every day. I told you my life was full.'

'And mine is empty,' I said savagely. 'You have made it empty, and now you must fill it...'

'I thought,' she said, smiling, 'that we had agreed that all that...'

'That's all nonsense,' I said. 'I don't care what we said, what we agreed upon; I cancel it all...'

'Well in that case,' she said, 'you know...'

'I don't know... I won't know...' I seized both her hands and pressed them violently.

I think she turned white.

'Don't, don't, don't,' she cried out, 'you are hurting me...'

She broke away from me.

'Listen to me one moment, like a reasonable being,' she said, 'for pity's sake... Jane Sedley is coming to take me out; now she will be here any minute, so do be careful; Jane is such a gossip.'

'I don't believe a word of it,' I said.

At that very moment Jane Sedley was announced. Jenny received her with sang-froid and said, 'At last. We thought you were never coming. Mr St Clair is coming back with us to Naples.'

I drove back with them and left them in the town. Godfrey came to dinner. He was very late. I expect he had been to say goodbye to Countess Zikov at the station.

We sat a long time at dinner and talked about old times. After dinner we sat on far into the night, drinking a delicious Neapolitan wine that had the colour of a fire opal. I told him about Charles, and began to tell him the whole of the rest of the story, as far as I was concerned in it, first of all in terms of *A* and *B*; but it was of no use. He knew me too well. I was obliged to drop all anonymity. I told him the whole truth.

His views were the same as the Abbé's, but for quite different reasons.

'I shouldn't bother about the young man,' he said. 'One can never prevent these things, and if one tries to prevent them, one always makes them worse. If he is left to himself, no harm will be done. Trust Jenny. She is very clever. You say she isn't in love with him. Let her manage the situation. It is a woman's business, not the work for our clumsy fingers ... but if I were you I would drop the whole thing. Go away, or "go to Rome", as Shelley says, or else you will burn *your* fingers. I don't know anything about this young man's work. It may be excellent, and if you say it is good, I am sure it is good. But I do know your work, and I think it would be a pity, a thousand pities, if anything interfered with that.'

'You mean,' I said, 'that I shall fall seriously in love with Jenny?'

'I think you *are* in love with her already,' he said, laughing, 'or if you are not, you will be soon, and you will find it out too late.'

'You think Jenny is so dangerous then?'

'No, not exactly dangerous ... but she is very, very ... *infectious*, and I think she likes you.'

'What nonsense!' I said.

Godfrey said it might well be nonsense. He had nothing really to go on. It was only his impression. Much as he liked Jenny, he had no illusions about her.

'You see,' he said, 'she is a person nobody can get rid of once they have had anything to do with her. She attracts men as candle-light attracts moths, even after they have been singed and burnt in the flame.'

'That's what Teresa says,' I said to him.

Godfrey asked me what Teresa thought about it all. I told him.

Godfrey said he entirely agreed with her. I told him what the Abbé said and he agreed with that.

'I come to exactly the same conclusions, although I start from the other pole,' he said, 'besides which, the Abbé is one of the shrewdest judges of human nature I have ever met, and he understands the world through and through and inside out, and men and women.'

I told Godfrey I couldn't go away and leave Charles here alone. Charles might arrive now at any moment.

'Then I am sure you *are* in love with Jenny,' he said, 'otherwise this mania for "saving" Charles at such immense risk to yourself is *inexplicable*. You must see that what was begun in the name of friendship with a man has grown into a passionate love for a woman. As for the young man, I don't think it would do him any harm.'

I denied that I was in love with Jenny, but Godfrey said the worst of it was that I was not even conscious of it and would not be till it was too late. I was deceiving myself.

I then returned to the charge about Charles. I told Godfrey that everything he said to me about Jenny applied to Charles in a higher degree. Why should I let him be burnt in the candle flame? I couldn't agree that it would do him no harm.

'There is all the difference in the world,' he said. 'Jenny doesn't care a pin for that artist, and she does care for you.'

I asked him how he could know. He had never set eyes on Charles, who was young, good-looking, attractive and bursting with talent and life.

'But I know Jenny,' he said, 'I have known her ever since she was fifteen years old. I don't care what the young man is like; I *know* she won't care for him ... not now at least.'

I said that Jenny was probably quite capable of deceiving him.

'She would never try to deceive me,' he said. 'She knows me far too well to care what I know, or don't know, about her. We have understood each other once and for all.'

'Very well,' I said, 'I will do as you say. I will not see Jenny again. Tomorrow I will telegraph to Teresa and ask her to stay on at Rome, and if Charles comes out we will try and keep him there. He is bound to pass through Rome.'

I didn't see Godfrey again, but the next morning I got a note from Jane Sedley asking me to dinner. I thought there was no harm in going there ... and it would look more natural, too. I did not want my departure to seem sudden. I dined with Jane, and there I met Jenny and sat next to her.

She was quiet and self-possessed. She talked a great deal about Godfrey. Wilfrid Harris sat on the other side of her and he seemed in the highest good humour as well, and was extremely civil to me.

Jenny asked after Charles in the most

natural way in the world. I had no talk with her after dinner, but before I left I asked her if she would be in at all the next day.

She said, 'No, not tomorrow, but the day after if...'

'If what?' I asked.

'You know,' she said, laughing, and I thought: 'She is playing with me the whole time. She turns us all round her little finger. Godfrey just as much as the rest of us, although he has known her ever since she was a child. However, she has at last found someone who is not taken in.' Then I thought to myself:

'Perhaps I am wrong after all. Perhaps there is no taking in at all about the matter. Perhaps my first idea and my first impressions were right after all ... one's first ideas generally are right... I know mine are, or at least I know my second thoughts are invariably wrong.

'Perhaps she is just playing the game and is expecting me to go on playing it and all that has happened so far has been according to rule and ritual. It simply means I have played correctly. It is I who am ignorant, inexperienced and clumsy, and don't know it.

'Thank heavens,' I said to myself, 'I shall still be in time to save Charles.'

I went to see her the next day, and the day after, and the day after that, and whether the game was played correctly I do not know, but I won. The queen was mine; my opponent resigned with joy.

And then I got a telegram from Teresa saying that she was coming back in two days' time, and Charles was coming with her.

CHAPTER 8

As soon as I felt that the game was won, I knew it had been lost.

Directly Teresa and Charles arrived I found that I was in an impossible situation. I realized first of all that there had been no game on the part of Jenny at all, as far as Charles was concerned, and as for her attitude towards myself I began to wonder whether the artifice had not been a product of my imagination. Charles went to see her directly he came back. He failed to see her the first time he went.

When she did see him it made matters worse, and he came back in a frenzy of despair. For three days I did not see Jenny, then I heard from her.

She told me she had had a terrible scene with Wilfrid Harris; he had told her she must choose between seeing me and him. I could guess, of course, what she had said. The consequence was he had left Naples. She begged me to come and see her. She did not even mention Charles.

I felt there was only one thing we could do, and that was to leave Naples.

I told Teresa that Jenny would not see Charles, and she could see the result for herself. He was almost insane. Teresa said nothing. I believe she understood everything. I said the only thing to be done was to go, leave Naples to go to Rome, to England, or anywhere.

Teresa agreed.

The lease of our villa came to an end at the end of the month. Nothing was more easy or more natural than for us to go away. To go away a fortnight sooner or later would make no difference. Teresa's sister was staying on in Rome for a little in our flat; that would be a good excuse for leaving. We could see her and then go back to England.

I went to see Jenny, to tell her what we had settled. First of all I told her about Charles: that he seemed to us like a man on the verge

111

of suicide.

'I know,' she said, 'I have seen him. It was all my fault ... I should never have had anything to do with him ... I never thought he cared, that he would care ... I thought he thought I was just ... well, just like anyone else ... now he cares quite dreadfully.'

She asked me what was to be done. I told her we had settled to leave Naples at once and to take Charles with us.

'And go away for good?' she said, 'to England?'

I said, 'Yes.'

'You can't go to England and leave me here alone?' she said. 'You can't do that, it will kill me.'

I asked her what she expected me to do ... what I was to say to Teresa ... what I was to do about Charles?

'Then,' she said, 'it's quite simple. You don't love me.'

I told her not to be absurd and to try and look at the matter from my point of view.

She thought a little, and then she said:

'I will believe you if you stay in Italy, just for this year. I don't care what you do afterwards. I agree we must separate for the moment. You can't stay on here at any rate, after the villa is let, and if you are to go it is perhaps better for you to go at once, much as that will hurt me ... but I only beg of you to stay in Italy, in Rome, just for this year. You were going to do that in any case. You have got a flat in Rome, go back to it and stay on there; if you do that, I can still believe that you love me, or that you loved me; if you go to England *now* I can never believe it, and it will kill me.'

I promised her I would stay in Rome.

She sat on the sofa with a white face, as if turned to stone. Had she often done this before? Was it all part of a regular ritual? I couldn't believe it. I believed she was sincere, or sincere for the time being ... I was certain of it, and I felt miserably ashamed and degraded ... it was I who had been playing a game, not she. For I (so I thought then) did not love her; never (so I thought then) had loved her.

We talked over the matter from every point of view.

What was to be done about Charles?

'He must never know,' said Jenny, 'you must take him to Rome. He will forget.'

'He won't forget,' I said.

'Yes, he will,' she said, 'people who love me forget almost at once ... you will forget ... very soon.'

She hurried me out of the house, as someone was coming to see her. She arranged that we should meet at the Museum the next day.

Then I went home and settled everything with Teresa.

We told Charles that we had to give up the villa, sooner than we had thought, as the owner was coming back. We were going back to our apartment in Rome for the present.

We were going at once, in two days' time.

Charles said he would stay on in Naples. We tried to dissuade him, but he was obdurate.

I met Jenny the next day at the Museum. She told me that she had settled to go to her aunt's, at Castellamare, and shut up her villa. She would come to Rome later. If we could, we must do something in the meanwhile about Charles; but she must see me once again before we left.

I told her it was difficult for me to go to her villa now without Charles knowing. She said if I came in the morning early, it would be all right. No one would know.

Charles was, as a matter of fact, far too distracted to pay heed to me or to my movements.

I went to see Jenny for the last time.

'I am going away tomorrow,' she said, 'and nobody will think it odd. I have constantly been to and fro to Castellamare. My aunt lives there. I always go there for the summer when Naples gets too hot. Wilfrid Harris has gone. People will think we have quarrelled ... and they will be right. Nobody will know the reason ... except perhaps Jane. I believe she has guessed.'

'I hope she won't make mischief,' I said, 'with Charles.'

'I don't think so,' said Jenny, 'she is a good sort at heart, and I believe she is fond of me. I have asked her to luncheon today on purpose. I have got twelve people to luncheon,' she laughed, 'my farewell luncheon, and it will go off well ... you see how well trained I am ... nobody will guess or suspect anything ... suspect that I am dying of sorrow, of inconsolable sorrow, for whatever happens, nothing can ever be the same again. But as long as you are in Rome, I shall have a spark of hope somewhere in my heart ... and all that matters is that Teresa and Charles should never know. It has all been my fault, but I loved you so much from the first moment I saw you. You are the only man I have ever loved in my life. How I like saying that,' she said, 'how wonderful it is to say those things when they are true. You said the same thing to me in a letter, but it wasn't true. Not then – you said it for fun ... and I knew it was for fun ... but I didn't mind because I thought you would get to love me when you knew me, and you did get to love me a little, didn't you? or has my love made me blind? You do love me a little now, don't you? Just a very very little? It is enough for me. How wonderful it was at first when you didn't care at all; you looked at me from such a long way off, so indifferent – like a man looking at someone through a telescope. I enjoyed it. I knew you would love me some day. I knew it was all difficult, impossible, and that it could never make for happiness. I realized all about Charles and Teresa and all the difficulties and the impossibilities, but I knew it would happen all the same, because I wanted it to happen so much. I *made* it happen. I forced it to happen. Because I couldn't live without your love, and I knew that if I wanted it so much, I must get it; and now it must come to an end, but not really to an end, not if you stay in Rome ... as long as you do that, I know everything will be all right. If I heard you had suddenly gone to England, then *that* would kill me. You do promise to stay in Rome at any rate for a year, for six months?'

I promised, and somehow my want of eloquence, for I was paralysed and tongue-tied, was, I believe, more convincing than any words might have been. I was overcome by what had happened, by the whole thing, and Jenny supplied the rest. She was quite confident for the time being. She felt I was hers for good and all, whatever might happen.

We said goodbye over and over again. It was nearly midday ... such a gorgeous day too ... there was the smell of Italian spring in the air ... not a cloud in the sky, songs, shouts, and laughter floating up from the distance and the noise of laughing life.

'You will write to me, just a line, even just a mark, every day,' she said. 'And I will write to you, to Mr D. *Poste restante*, Rome ... you will go and fetch the letters ... or if you feel Teresa's hidden sense is minding that, I won't send any letters at all, I will write and post my letters in the sea, but they will be written all the same.'

I told her I would never forget her... I poured out a torrent of words. They all seemed true at the moment, but I thought then that in reality they were not true, and that if she had been less blinded at the moment, she would have known. She – I said

– supplied all the gaps in what I said, all that was wanting. If it was all true, how could I leave Naples? That is what I said to myself.

And at last, the moment for the very last goodbye came. We walked through the garden, past the orange trees.

She picked a white rose and gave it to me, and I thought as she walked through the garden of how she had posed that night as Flora leading on the spring... 'Why could I not love her,' I said to myself, 'as she loved me?' I could admire her, wonder at her, delight in her, but I could not feel about her – so I said to myself then – even what I still felt about Teresa, that I could not live without her ... she was a beautiful accessory to life, something gratuitous ... but not something to me indispensable. I thought it was because she loved me too much, I could only love those who didn't love me enough – so I said then.

We walked right down to the sea and back, and the final goodbye was silent. She stood as she watched me going, white and calm as a statue ... again like one of those poses she had done: Dido watching Aeneas leaving Africa ... and I wondered whether she had often done this before, convinced as I was now that she was for the moment sincere ...

but I still thought of her as a *light* woman, a woman to whom these dramas are daily occurrences, necessities like food and drink ... I was certain she was sincere for the time, but that she would forget it all in a day or two, and in six months be enacting the same part with someone else ... that is what prevented me from having more compunction.

I walked from Posilippo to the town. I had some shopping to do. In the distance the hills of Sorrento were like Keats' light blue hills. Vesuvius was dormant, but capped with a little snowy cloud. The hills inland were bright with their fresh spring apparel. Mules and donkey carts passed me laden with vegetables: carrots, turnips, cabbages, onions ... their huge white and green parasols open wide... Charcoal sellers were shouting, tramcars whistled and passed shrieking by; men and boys were singing. Everything was hot, dusty, loud, bright and gay. It was the spring. The Italian spring.

When I got home, Teresa told me that Charles still refused to leave Naples. He said he would stay on at the hotel. The next day he heard that Jenny had left for Castellamare. At least I suppose he did. He never mentioned Jenny to us, nor we her to him.

Then we left for Rome. Charles refused to

come with us, but said he would perhaps follow us in a day or two. He had some work he had to finish at Naples.

We settled ourselves in our apartment in Rome. My son, Harry, came out for his Easter holidays and stayed a fortnight. Teresa's sister was still there. Her husband had gone to Cairo, but she was waiting till their house there would be ready. She was staying in our flat.

To my surprise I found Godfrey Law still in Rome. He had changed his plans. He was not going to London after all. He had been offered the post of First Secretary in Rome, which had suddenly become vacant, and he had accepted it.

I wondered whether Countess Zikov had anything to do with this, and whether they were still going to London. I heard, a few days later, that it was probable they were going to London, but not for six months at any rate, or even possibly a year.

They were in Rome now. Three days later, Charles came to Rome. He had evidently found it impossible to see anything of Jenny at Castellamare. And he was still like a being who belonged to another world.

He walked about like a somnambulist. He seemed neither to see nor to hear. He lived in his studio and did apparently a certain amount of work, mechanically painting from the model ... but he never talked of it, and he showed us nothing.

I dined with Godfrey one night, and he asked me what had happened about Jenny.

'Nothing,' I said, 'that's all over. She went away to Castellamare, and left us all.'

'That's the best that could happen,' he said, 'I expect she went to meet young Gallazzi, he has relations who live at Castellamare. I hear that she is desperately in love with him, and they say that Wilfrid Harris found out all about it and was so furious that he left Jenny. He has gone back to London.'

'Really?' I said.

I believed what Godfrey said to be true, difficult as it was to believe, that she had played a comedy so tragically. But Godfrey knew her very well, and he was a man who did not deal in false gossip. He was generally right. He never took the second-hand superficial view.

I said to him, 'You know Gallazzi?'

'Very well.'

'And, knowing Jenny as you do, you think she is in love with him?'

'Jenny,' he said, 'cares enormously for

looks and youth, and she understands and likes foreigners, and especially Italians; the southern temperament. Englishmen are too old and too heavy for her. I don't mean just too old in years. That has nothing to do with it. But Jenny is as light as a butterfly, and she needs a southern flower to rest on, and southern sunshine. Wilfrid, poor Wilfrid, has always been devoted to her, but he is far too old and far too heavy for her.'

'Then,' I said, 'I wonder she wasn't fonder of Charles, considering how passionately devoted he was to her, and is still.'

'Oh, that's not Jenny's affair,' he said, 'artists and writers, I beg your pardon, Horace, bore Jenny really to death. The fact of the matter is, they are too selfish. She likes people who are devoted to her, and devoted to her day and night, the whole time, who are ready to give her every moment of their lives.'

'But Charles,' I said, 'would be ready to give her every moment of his life, I am sure of it.'

'But that's not the kind of life Jenny wants given to her,' he said. 'Jenny must be amused. She's light, and she wants some-thing light back. She doesn't want to play ping-pong with cannon-balls.'

'But all the same,' I said, 'she has some-times pretended to be pleased with heavier metal.'

'Oh Jenny,' he said, 'never throws admir-ation away ... not at first, at any rate. She can't resist it. It's her second nature.'

'But she gets tired of it after a time?'

'Yes – in a way, not exactly tired, but she has enough – and once it's over, it's over for ever.'

I thought of all the short passionate letters that I fetched every day from the *Poste rest-ante*. They seemed to have the very accent of sincerity. I wondered women, any woman, could take the trouble to waste so much pow-der and shot, and all for nothing. I supposed Godfrey was right; it was their second nature.

Up to that moment I had written to her every day. But now I felt I had been fooled enough. I would stop writing.

The fourth day after I had stopped writ-ing, I received a telegram from Castellamare saying:

'What is the matter, coming Rome.'

CHAPTER 9

Jenny's telegram was followed by a letter in which she told me that her old friend, Mary Boldoni, an Englishwoman who had married an Italian, was going to England for the summer and wanted to let her flat. She asked Jenny whether she could find her a tenant. Jenny had at once said she would take the flat herself, and she was coming to Rome immediately to take possession.

The day I received this letter Charles came to see me in the morning. He was not staying with us. He was living in his own studio.

He walked about my room saying nothing for a time, smoking; at last he spoke, and in speaking he seemed to be exercising immense self-control.

'I've got something to say to you, and it's this. I think Teresa and you have been interfering in my affairs in an unwarrantable way – and I don't think it's fair. I think it's unpardonable. It's got to stop.'

I said I didn't understand what he meant.

He then went on to say, his voice and his

hands shaking with suppressed passion, that we had put an end to his friendship with Jenny.

'You have treated me like a child,' he said; 'it's no good denying it. I know it for a fact. You have both of you asked Jenny not to have anything to do with me. But you don't understand ... neither of you.'

I said I knew Jenny far too little to venture to offer her any advice on any subject.

'Teresa knows her well,' he said, 'she is one of Jenny's oldest friends. Jenny adores her and goes entirely by what she says.'

I said it was quite true that Teresa had at one moment thought it would be a pity if Charles had got into the habit of living in rather an idle, demoralizing world, as she attached ... (and so did I) ... so much importance to his work ... and that sort of life was the end of work...

'And so you thought seeing Jenny would prevent me working?'

'No, not seeing *her*,' I said.

'And what do you think *not* seeing her does?' he asked, savagely. 'Do you think I have done any work, any serious work, since I have stopped seeing her? I don't understand you and Teresa. Do you think I wanted to enjoy a mild flirtation, and to play a game of spillikins? I wanted – and I still want – to marry Jenny... I mean to marry her, if it is humanly possible, and I shall marry her, whatever you may say and do. You and Teresa have been treating me as if I were a child. You think I know nothing. You think I have been taken in by Jenny. But the truth is, you neither of you know Jenny, not as I know her. You know her as the world knows her. You think that is Jenny. But I know her as she really is, as God knows her. Don't laugh. I was never more serious in my life. For heaven's sake don't think that I have been taken in, deceived, made a fool of... Jenny told me everything. I know her whole life... I know everything that has happened to her. She never encouraged me. She did everything to put me off.'

'Then she told you she couldn't marry you?' I interrupted.

'She was bound to say that at first,' said Charles, 'because she didn't think that I should go on wanting to marry her. She thought that what I was feeling was just a *coup de tête*, but I would have convinced her. I was convincing her. I was bound to convince her. Everything was going well, till I went away and until you and Teresa meddled.'

'Teresa never meddled,' I said. 'On the contrary.'

'Well, then *you* did. I know it. I know it from what Jenny said.'

'What did she say?'

'She said – she says *now* that she could never marry me, that she would ruin my career as an artist – as if that mattered.'

'But didn't she always say that?'

'Yes, but now she says it differently. She has been quite different ever since I went away.'

I told Charles he was mad to think that anyone had interfered ... that anyone would ever dream of interfering with his life. I was certain, too, that nobody could influence Jenny. That she knew her own mind, I was sure. That if she said she could not marry him, she meant it.

'Yes, but at first she didn't say it like that,' he kept on repeating. 'It was different. Everything was different.'

'What do you want us to do now?' I asked.

'Nothing,' he said, 'only not to interfere, not to tell Jenny she would ruin my career if she married me.'

'But does she want to marry you?' I asked.

'She may not now, but she might ... she will ... when she sees how serious I am ... what it really means to me ... how it will ruin my life if she doesn't...'

'You can't force those things,' I said. 'You can't make people love and marry those they don't want to love and marry.'

'Oh! But you don't know ... you don't understand,' said Charles. 'It was all so different before ... she might have been fond of me ... she was growing fond of me...'

I said I supposed his absence had given her time to think over things, and to look into herself.

'No,' he said, 'it's something else. Something that has made her change her mind. Something from the outside. I felt it directly I came back. And I am sure it is something to do with Teresa and you. Even if you said nothing, Jenny knew you both disapproved. I know she is afraid of ruining my career. She doesn't understand that she will ruin it if she doesn't marry me.'

I said I thought Jenny's life was full already.

'You don't understand... All that doesn't count, all that never has counted; all those Italians ... they meant nothing ... nothing at all.'

Then he startled me by saying that Jenny was coming to Rome.

'Has she told you?' I asked.

He had not heard that from Jenny. He had met a friend of Countess Boldoni's who had told him Jenny had taken the flat.

'You must persuade Jenny,' he said, 'you and Teresa, that it would be all right.'

I told Charles that he was out of his mind. We couldn't interfere ... we couldn't say anything... It was preposterous... 'Besides which,' I said, 'I think it would be useless ... I don't think she *will* marry you ... I don't think she will marry anyone.'

'Well, all I ask you and Teresa – and especially Teresa, is not to do anything against it...'

'Teresa will do nothing,' I said.

'Nor you?'

'I am not sure I do think it would be a good thing,' I said, 'for you to marry Jenny True.'

'There, I knew it!' he said. 'It's *you* who have prevented it!'

I saw that whatever I said would only make everything worse, so I said:

'If Jenny True says she will marry you, I swear not to lift a finger to try and prevent it ... besides, how could I? What would be the use?'

I felt pretty safe in saying this, because I thought that whatever might happen, Jenny would not want to marry Charles. Then he left me, and I was in a state of great perplexity.

I was bewildered. What had Jenny done? What part had she played? What part was she playing now? If I only knew, if I could only tell for certain. She had certainly, I was sure, never meant to marry Charles. She seemed to have given him up, but had she given him up? What did her coming to Rome mean? Did it mean that she was going to give up nothing? Neither Charles nor myself nor Wilfrid? Wilfrid was still at the Grand Hotel ... waiting, no doubt... She was unfathomable ... but if this was so, then Charles must be delivered from her ... but how...? It was all too late ... everything seemed to me in a hopeless tangle.

Teresa came in presently, and said to me:

'Jenny is coming to Rome.'

'I know,' I said. 'Charles has been here; he told me.'

'All Rome has heard of it,' said Teresa. 'It was Godfrey Law who told me ... he is delighted ... what did Charles say?'

I told Teresa more or less what Charles had said.

'Charles is right,' she said; 'we must at all costs not interfere.'

'But have we interfered?'

'God knows I haven't,' said Teresa. And she left me.

I wondered what Teresa was thinking, and how much she really knew.

That afternoon I met Jane Sedley in the street. She said to me, with a knowing air:

'Jenny True is coming to live in Rome ... for the whole summer...'

I told her I had heard the news.

'Yes,' she said, 'and a great many people will be pleased, especially Gallazzi ... his mother will be furious. She thinks Jenny is ruining his life... I must say I feel for her.'

'Does Mrs True see a great deal of him?' I asked.

'Morning, noon and night,' she said.

I wondered how much truth there was in this – I didn't quite believe it, but I didn't disbelieve it. And then I wondered whether the Abbé's prophecies were coming true, and whether Jenny, suspecting that I had wished to detach her from Charles, was about to capture him seriously and once for all. What a mistake I had made to try and take part in this drama at all! How right Teresa had been! How right the Abbé had been! How right everyone had been, except myself! There was nothing to be done now but to wait. Things might grow better ... but they couldn't very well be worse.

We didn't hear of Charles for a day or two. Then Godfrey Law asked us to dinner. He was living in a flat he had taken, but he had not yet got his things into it. We went, and the first person I saw when I came into the room was Jenny.

Gallazzi was not there ... nor Wilfrid Harris, but some colleagues of Godfrey's, and the Abbé.

I did not sit next to Jenny, but I had an opportunity of talking to her after dinner.

I asked her why she had come to Rome.

'Don't you know?' she asked quite seriously.

I said I had no idea... I had gone back to the light tone of the beginning of our acquaintance when I was convinced that we were both of us playing a game.

'I came,' she said slowly, 'because I could not live another day without seeing you.'

'Is that what you say to Gallazzi?' I said.

Jenny turned white and looked as if I had cut her with a whip. She looked in front of her at a clock, as if she were slowly spelling the time.

'Oh! You are unkind!' she whispered...

'I didn't mean anything ... I only thought perhaps...'

Godfrey came up and asked Jenny to play bridge. In the course of the evening somone mentioned the name of Gallazzi.

'He's gone away,' Jenny said, 'to shoot big game in Africa. He will be away some months.'

'Ah! *La chasse aux lions,*' said the Abbé.

The next morning I got a note from Jenny asking me to come and see her between five and six. I found her alone.

She gave me tea, and then she said:

'I know you think it's awful of me to have come here after all that has happened, and after all that I told you. But I haven't changed my mind ... nothing has altered ... I mean, I don't want to see you more than I would see you anyhow, if we were just friends ... only I must be in the same place ... I must see you – every now and then – I ask nothing ... I shall never ask you to come and see me ... or to do anything... We will meet at other people's houses, just as we should meet naturally ... there will be nothing odd about it ... no one will notice anything; only I shall be in the same place as you are ... I shall see you from time to time. I want you to know the truth. I feel that you don't quite understand.'

'I don't think I do,' I said satirically.

'That's just it,' she said, 'will you never

understand...? Do men never understand anything – and you a clever man?'

'Some problems, and some people,' I said, 'are very difficult.'

'Well, then,' she said, 'perhaps I had better explain.'

She paused a little, and then she said:

'What is the use of explanations? I suppose you know what there is to be known ... I suppose you know, you must know, what I feel for you, unless you are made of iron and ice, unless you are blind, deaf, hard, cased up in wax and steel ... muffled, watertight ... but you do know, you did know ... or are you just jealous, Horace ... just jealous of Alfredo Gallazzi – or someone?'

'Yes, just jealous,' I said, and my listless accent lent conviction to my words.

'Oh!' she said, and her face lit up with a celestial smile of happiness. 'That's too good to be true.'

Then I saw my opportunity.

I said: 'I'm only jealous of one person, nobody you think. Not of Gallazzi, I never really gave him a thought.'

'Who?' she said. 'Wilfrid?'

'Oh, no!' I laughed.

'Then who?'

'Charles,' I said, and I wondered as I said

it whether it was not perhaps true.

'Charles! Surely not Charles! But I thought we were agreed about Charles ... you know he wanted to marry me. To *marry* me! To marry *me!*'

'Yes, and now he thinks Teresa and I have prevented it.'

'Oh!' she said. 'Well, you have, in a way, but not in the way he thinks.'

'Did you ever think of marrying him?'

'Oh, no! I would never have married him, poor boy, not him nor anyone... But what shall we do?'

'I have no idea,' I said. 'The fact of your being here will be enough to keep him here for ever.'

'You want me to go,' said Jenny. 'I can't. Don't ask me. I needn't see you, except when we meet in the world... I won't see you. Never. I won't even write to you, now that I'm here... But I must *be* here... I won't, I can't go ... or I will if you like, only it will kill me ... really kill me ... you know people really die of such things.' She laughed. 'Do you know,' she added, 'I knew someone, an old lady, who died of a broken heart because she had acted the part of Hamlet's mother badly at some private theatricals.'

Jenny laughed, and I laughed, too. She said:

'I might have died of that too, although that's different... But about Charles. I think I will see him and talk to him sensibly.'

'That will be fatal,' I said.

'Well, I think I had better see him once, and, after that, I won't see him.'

'You must explain to him,' I said, 'that the reason you are not marrying him is not because you are afraid of ruining his career – that it's nothing to do with his art.'

'Yes, of course,' she said.

'You see, he thinks it's a matter of time; he is under the delusion that he will bring you round and persuade you in the end.'

'I know. Leave it to me; I think I can manage it. Now you must go. But I don't want you to think that I am under an illusion. Not a great illusion. I mean, I know what I mustn't expect; but I do think that you love me a little ... perhaps that, too, is an illusion.'

And then I knew, at that moment, that I had been wrong from the beginning to the end... I knew that she had never given a thought to Charles ... that Gallazzi might have been one in a million... I knew it had never been ... would never be ... a game. I knew I had been wrong – blind, deaf, thick-witted, asinine, pompous, conceited, vain, shallow, ridiculous ... a peacock without the excuse of his plumage, and yet it was not all conceit. I had never believed that a woman like Jenny could love something so drab as myself ... and I thought, too, that I couldn't make things any better – now ... that I didn't – so I said to myself then – when all was said and done, *love* Jenny ... not as she loved me... I had made a hash of things... I had played a game with fatal results, and she hadn't... I had not only played, but organized, the *sombre comédie* which the Abbé had spoken of ... what was to be done now? Nothing. There could be nothing, except retribution and punishment and the inevitable result of one's own folly...

I left Jenny, and I shall never forget the moment when I left her. She was standing up against an empty fireplace in the high square room of the apartment, which was on the ground floor. She was dressed in white, but her face and her hands were whiter than her clothes... She seemed to have grown thinner than when I last saw her ... her hands seemed thinner ... her eyes larger and softer. They had grey, not rings, but shadows under them. They were as soft as the hills of Sorrento and as blue, that delicate light blue ... but the laughter had gone from them. They were infinitely sad and serious ... but I mustn't anticipate.

Even now, at this supreme moment, I did not really understand. I knew that Jenny had not been playing a game with me, but I didn't understand what kind of woman Jenny was. I still thought that she was a *light* woman, who had been momentarily and unconsciously hoist with her own petard. But I thought it meant nothing really ... that it was a sentimental episode in the life of a woman who had had a thousand such sentimental episodes and who would have a thousand more.

I did not think the matter was really serious, really important... I knew that she was not just angling for me, Charles, the Italian, and others ... but I thought that I was as one particular kind of fish is for a fisherman, interesting at the moment of its catching ... that when the sport was over, however serious it might be at the time, however sincere her fisherman's passion might be, it would be instantly forgotten, when the day was over and the next day's fishing began.

I knew she was really, truly and sincerely engrossed for the moment in the catching, or in the landing, or in having caught and landed this particular fish ... for the moment nothing else counted ... nothing in the world; but I was convinced that it would all soon be forgotten, and that she would go out gaily on the morrow after other fry; some perhaps smaller, some perhaps larger, according to the weather, the flies she had with her, and the mood of the moment.

CHAPTER 10

Jenny was as good as her word. She made no effort to see me. Another chapter of life began, and life seemed to have slipped back into its usual groove, as if nothing had happened; and yet everything was different. There seemed to be a subtle difference in the sunlight itself. I felt this, but I didn't realise or face the reason. I was still deceiving myself. Charles was by way of working ... we saw him often, not so often as before, but when we did see him, he never alluded to what happened. I thought he looked ill. I suspected him of not doing any work, and I am sure Teresa felt the same, although she said nothing.

We began to make plans for the future. We settled to stay in Rome until the end of June;

after that, to avoid the heat, we thought of the Tyrol or the Vosges for a month or two, somewhere where Harry could amuse himself. Teresa had to do a cure first; we meant to come back to Rome for the autumn and the winter, and to keep on our apartment.

Teresa wanted to go back to London, but, remembering my promise to Jenny, I said that it would be impossible for me to do any work in London. This was not really true, as I was doing no work as it was, although I was pretending to.

We saw a great deal of Godfrey Law. He was quite settled in Rome now.

The Zikovs were there too, and we heard nothing beyond a vague rumour of their going to London.

I did not say a word to Godfrey about the situation, and he asked no questions.

Every now and then we met Jenny at his house, but not more often than we met other people. He must have known or felt what had happened. Perhaps Jenny had told him. She saw him constantly ... perhaps she asked him not to ask us too often to meet her ... he certainly didn't. His apartment was small, and he could not have more than six people to dinner, and he was certainly more than ever engrossed with Countess

140

Zikov. The Zikovs were always invited, and everybody took it as a matter of course.

I saw Godfrey often. We talked about everything in the world except Jenny, and Jenny saw him often, almost every day ... so Jane Sedley told me ... and she added that he ought to be careful, as Countess Zikov was beginning to get jealous. I laughed when she told me this, little knowing how serious it might prove to be.

One day Teresa said to me: 'I saw Charles yesterday; we met by chance at the Capitol. I think he is looking better. I believe Jenny has made him see the thing in a sensible way. I believe he is working.'

I told Teresa I would make sure, and the next day I went round to Charles' studio. He had begun rather a large picture from a model. It seemed to be promising.

He talked a little about his work. I mentioned Teresa's portrait, and asked if he could not go on with it, but he said it was quite impossible. The picture was a failure. I began to argue with him, but I soon saw it was quite useless.

We talked of other things, and I realized perhaps for the first time how much things had changed in our relations. He was quite friendly, but he seemed miles away ... like a man in another world. I don't think ... in fact, I am sure, he had no grievance or grudge against me at this moment, but he had slipped away from the world in which we used to meet, and the things we had been used to discuss together no longer interested him ... he was thinking of something else the whole time ... he was somewhere else. Jenny? Yes, but what had she done? What had she told him? I had not seen her alone, nor had I had any private conversation with her, since the first time I had been to see her after her return to Rome.

Then one evening Jane Sedley gave a large dinner at the Grand Hotel, to which we went... Jenny was there, and Wilfrid Harris, and Adderly, Godfrey Law, and Charles. I was put next to Jenny, but she paid little attention to me and talked almost incessantly to her neighbour, an oldish Italian, a professor of archaeology.

After dinner she talked to Godfrey for the rest of the evening.

Charles talked to Teresa at dinner and to Jane Sedley afterwards.

The next morning early, before I had finished dressing, and before I had drunk my coffee, Charles burst into my room. He was like a madman.

'I know everything,' he said.

I asked him what he meant.

'You have taken Jenny from me,' he said. 'That is the last thing I thought would happen, and you took advantage of my absence to do it. It's the meanest thing you could have done – that anyone could have done.'

I laughed, and told him what nonsense I thought he was talking ... how Teresa and I seldom saw Jenny...

'Then why has she come to Rome?' he asked.

I said I really didn't know; he must ask her; but there was nothing odd about it, considering Jenny had lived for years in Rome, and had nearly always spent the winter there.

'The winter!' he said. 'That's just it, but the summer!'

I said I had heard she was going back to Naples for the summer. The summer hadn't really begun.

'I do think you are a bad friend,' he went on, 'to take her from me; of course, it was easy for you, child's play, with your "fame" and "reputation", to take her away from someone who has nothing to show – worse than nothing; beginnings; promise.'

I told him he was being unfair to Jenny; and that if he thought she was the sort of woman who couldn't resist the glamour of a fleeting notoriety – well, then, she was hardly worth caring about.

'That's all rot,' he said. 'You know quite well no woman can resist that sort of thing, when people like you make up to them ... they can't resist the market value of people, and your market value is worldwide and world-high at present – whereas mine is *nil*.'

I laughed, and said I didn't think that Jenny was deeply interested in art or literature.

'No,' he said, 'that's just it, but she *is* interested in what other people think of art and literature, and she knows the whole world thinks your art good, and they have never heard of mine ... and she thinks my pictures are bad, not because she thinks so herself – she thinks nothing – but because other people have told her so ... probably you yourself among them.'

Then I got angry and asked him if he really thought I had told anybody his pictures were bad. It was too unfair – monstrous.

'Oh! Not in so many words; but you have implied it.'

I said that was a lie. The tone of the discussion altered, and he became bitter, then disagreeable, then violent. We both of us lost our tempers, and finally I refused to discuss the matter any longer.

'It's no good your saying anything,' Charles shrieked out in a passion of rage. 'The whole world knows that you have taken Jenny from me ... that you are a disloyal thief – everyone knows it. You see her every day, she sees nobody else but you.'

I swore to him I had only seen Jenny once since she had come to Rome.

'Jane Sedley,' he said, 'talked about it as a matter of course; she told me that when I was away you used to go to Jenny's villa every day... It was the talk ... the joke of Naples.'

'Jane is a world-famous gossip,' I said. 'Besides which, she was pulling your leg. She revels in that kind of joke.'

'Yes, but her gossip and her jokes are generally founded on fact.'

'She told me,' I said, 'that Jenny was going to marry Gallazzi, and he has gone to Abyssinia or somewhere to shoot big game.'

'Yes, he has probably gone on account of you, because you took Jenny away from him... He saw he had no chance.'

I laughed bitterly and told Charles he was raving mad.

'I think,' he said, slowly and deliberately, 'that what you have done is the worst thing a man can do to anyone ... nothing you can say or do will make me disbelieve it. I feel it is true – I feel it in my bones. One had only to look at Jenny when she said how-do-you-do to you last night, to see it was true.

'And what makes it worse is that you don't *really* love her; although you may think you do – and you don't appreciate her. You have no notion what Jenny is like, what Jenny *is*. *You don't know Jenny*. You never can know Jenny, because you are too conceited, too vain. You are a sham ... your life is a sham and your art is a sham. You are like the man who, when he was alone in a room, vanished; when somebody looked through the key hole there was no one there to see. Isn't that a story by Henry James or someone? The whole of your art is nothing ... nothing. It has been made popular by a fluke because by accident you happened to chance on a subject that made a good libretto, and you have been lifted into fame on the wings of light opera. You are utterly and completely selfish. You only love yourself ... that is why your art is bad and always will be bad, however popular it may be, however "famous" you may be or become for the moment. You are unreal. You have never touched life. Jenny is real, and that is why you can't understand Jenny. You are not worthy to touch her shoestrings.'

I let him finish his tirade, then I said:

'That is all probably true – all that you say about my art; but don't you think it is Jenny in all this whom you are underrating? Why should you think her so foolish to be taken in by so utterly worthless a person? After all, she is a clever woman, and she has had a lot of experience.'

'It is just because she is so true and so genuine that she is taken in by a flat-catcher like you,' he said. 'That always happens. She has seen my pictures, and she honestly dislikes them, but she has never read your books, and she will never read them ... there you have the advantage ... she will never know...'

'How bad they are,' I interrupted. 'You usedn't always to think they were so bad,' I added, 'or if you did – you didn't say so – you usedn't to imply I was a flat-catcher.'

'When I say *bad*, I mean that relatively; of course, I know they are clever, and above the average, and well-written ... very good, if you like, compared with the stuff that is poured out every day ... with all the stuff that sells, but compared with real art ... with excellence ... with greatness ... with something like Balzac or Flaubert or Tourgenev ... well, you know as well as I do that none of your work will live, not a line of it.'

'You are right there,' I said. 'Not a line of it.'

'In spite of your European reputation.'

'In spite of my "European" reputation ... but what has that got to do with it?'

'It's got everything to do with it,' said Charles. 'All that reputation is so much glamour: assets. Jenny can't help thinking you are the kind of person the world thinks you to be ... she can't resist the glamour ... the halo.'

'You don't give her credit for much intelligence, or for any independence, then?'

'I give her credit for human nature. She wouldn't be human if she didn't feel that.'

I told him I thought he was really making an imaginary picture of Jenny; that she had never said a word to me about my books. I didn't know if she had ever read them.

'Of course she hasn't read them,' he said, 'that's the whole point.'

'How can it be the point?'

'Oh, you understand nothing,' Charles said, 'in spite of being a psychologist ... perhaps because you are a psychologist ... nothing ... nothing at all. However, we needn't discuss that ... the fact remains that you have stolen Jenny from me ... if it hadn't been for you, she would have married me.'

'Really, Charles,' I said, 'that's too much. I can stand a good deal, but not that.'

'You laugh because you don't know ... you haven't the faintest idea of what Jenny thought or thinks or of anything...'

'Then what is the use of arguing with me?' I asked.

'I agree there is no use ... no use in it whatsoever ... only I wanted you to know once and for all what I thought of you, and I wanted to tell you that our friendship is at an end, and why it is at an end.'

'In a week's time you will be the first to laugh at all this,' I said.

'You'll see,' he said, 'and what's more, Teresa agrees with me.'

'Have you talked to Teresa?'

'No, but I can see she does. Teresa sees everything – she knows.'

I remained perfectly calm, and I tried to argue with Charles. I was matter of fact, reasonable, persuasive, convincing. I didn't get heated. I was slow, ponderous, logical, explanatory. I simply said the whole thing was absurd and the result of an overexcited brain.

'You are in love with Jenny, and because she doesn't love you as much as you love her,' I said, 'you imagine everything.'

Charles laughed bitterly.

'Imagine!' he said. 'It is you writers who talk glibly of imagination...! You imagine things and situations easily enough in your books: combinations, crises, scenes, curtains; but when it comes to understanding the simple motives of any human heart your imagination fails you ... you can imagine nothing then ... you can't even imagine what is there, staring you in the face, the sort of thing that a woman like Jenny feels, and is bound to feel ... you are so used to judging things by the standards of literature and books, of fiction and falsity, that you get anything to do with life utterly and completely wrong. You become blind – life-blind.'

'That's all very well,' I said, 'but you forget that you too are an artist, Charles.'

'That's different,' he said. 'I just paint what I see, and I have no theories whatsoever, except that one should try and paint well and not badly, one should try and draw a straight line straight and put the paint on the canvas in the right quantity and in the right place.'

'That is the only theory I have,' I said.

'It's not the only theory you express,' he said.

'Expressions of theories in books,' I said,

'are like the lines and colours in your pictures; they are only a part of the material of the work of art.'

'Yes,' he said, 'but the fact of expressing theories in books makes you have wrong theories about life ... it prevents you from seeing people as they really are...'

I said I couldn't go on discussing these things ... we were weaving theories in this discussion. I could only tell him over and over again that he was talking nonsense and behaving like a foolish, silly child ... a spoilt, naughty child. It was *polissonnerie*.

'However,' I ended by saying, 'Teresa and I are leaving Rome soon, at the end of the month; we are going to the Vosges, so you needn't see anything of us or hear of us again.'

Then he blazed up in a final burst of rage:

'That doesn't prevent your having done what you have done,' he said, 'and it's irrevocable. It can't be undone. You have ruined my life ... and I'm not sure you haven't ruined Jenny's life too.'

He went out of the room and banged the door. That door bang had the sound of fate to me.

Teresa came in when he had left and asked what was the matter. She had heard the noise of the discussion and the door banging.

I gave her an account of what Charles had said; a completely truthful account.

'Yes,' Teresa said; 'you see, we shouldn't have meddled.'

I was greatly struck and immensely upset by everything Charles had said to me. There was so much truth in it, and the truth was all the more striking from the falsity of the angle at which it was presented.

I felt to blame, very much to blame ... only Charles didn't know my motives ... he couldn't know them, or even dimly guess ... and then all that he said about Jenny – was that true? There, too, there was a small grain of truth that was not pleasant...

Teresa was right; we should never have meddled ... that is to say, I should never have meddled.

I looked at the last chapter of the MS I was engaged upon. I read it through. It was very good 'St Clair'; the phrases sounded just right. I could see in my mind's eye what the reviewers would say about it. 'Mr St Clair's inimitable style', 'his delicate subtle touch', 'usual distinction', and then Charles' words, 'sham, all sham', echoed in my mind. I threw the MS into the fire.

CHAPTER 11

The day after Charles' visit I received a long letter from him.

'You know me too well,' he wrote, 'not to know that I never meant, that I could not mean, half of what I said. I was not sane at the time. I am not sane now, but sane enough to know that all that I said about you as an artist, all that I said about your *work*, was not true. I never meant it, and I never thought it – not a word of it ... all those black words came welling out at a demon's prompting... You know what I think about your work ... you know that in praising it and appreciating it I have always been sincere ... you know how much it has influenced me ... what I said was not only insane but silly, for if it had been true, I should have no grievance. The contrary is true ... only perhaps the truth is worse ... it is the *merit* of your work that has taken Jenny from me ... she may never read your books – but that has nothing to do with it. It is the fact that you

153

are able to write them. You had only to know her, however little, and there was no more chance for me. I do not altogether blame you ... it is not entirely your fault. I suppose you cannot help being yourself. Jenny cannot help being herself... I do not accuse you of deliberate treachery, but I do think that when you saw what has happened was likely to happen, and beginning to happen, you might have stopped in time. I suppose it was then already too late. You were too fond of her already. But even then I do think that you might, just out of loyalty to me, have tried to sacrifice what was, after all, not yet a serious passion – it can't have been – and put an end to the whole thing. But what is the use of discussing this now? The fact, the sad fact, remains that consciously or unconsciously you have taken Jenny away from me ... even if you never see her again, this is so, and cannot be otherwise ... and this has cut the cord of our friendship with a knife ... there is nothing more to be said or done. Forget, if you can, all the things I said about your art, they were the mean words that are born of anger and jealousy. I say forget, I do not ask you to forgive, because I can't forgive you.'

I wrote back to him and told him that he

was really insane. That I thought that all he had said about my work only too true. I was well aware that in his youthful enthusiasm he had put me on a pedestal, and that I had warned him myself that a day would come when he would see the idol he had set up as it really was, he would see me as I was, and that then he would suffer a great disappointment. I knew – so I told him – this was bound to happen sooner or later.

When I read his letter, convinced as I was of his sincerity, I still thought what he said about my work was true ... although I believed that he no longer thought so now. And yet I was less to blame than he thought ... if he had known the truth. Where I had been to blame was interfering at all. No motive, however good, can make wrong right, and I had done wrong. And now we were both paying for it.

I saw Godfrey daily, and through him I had news of Jenny. And I think she saw him constantly so as to have news of me. She was going to stay on in Rome till the end of July; then she, too, would go north somewhere, for a while, and then come back to Rome. Godfrey was not going away at all ... he might get leave for a month, perhaps, and go to Aix-les-Bains, or somewhere, it depended on a number of things.

At the end of the month, Teresa and I left for France. We went first to a watering-place called Hareville, where Teresa took the waters for three weeks and I tried to work, but I accomplished nothing. I was stuck in the middle of a serious book, and I was disgusted with it and could not go on.

After Teresa had finished her cure we went to a small place in the mountains for a *Nachkur*. Our boy joined us in August and stayed with us till the end of the holidays. Charles remained in Rome. I heard nothing from him, but Godfrey wrote to me and told me that he was said to be working hard.

Godfrey wrote to me at least once a week and told me all the news.

The Zikovs were staying on at Rome. Jane Sedley had gone. Jenny was going to the Mont Dore, and he was going to join her there, as he had been suffering from a sore throat and asthma, and the doctor said he must have a cure.

Then I heard from him at the Mont Dore.

Jenny had arrived, and Wilfrid Harris had gone back to England. Godfrey thought there had been a final row. In any case, Jenny would not let him come to the Mont Dore with her. He was enjoying himself.

Jenny herself never wrote to me.

Towards the end of September we went back to Rome. Teresa wanted to go to London, but I said I could not face London at present. She did not press the point. She just accepted my decision. I found Godfrey in Rome. He gave me news of Charles. He had been in Rome, or in the environs, all the summer, and had been supposed to be working, but whether he had accomplished anything or not, Godfrey had no idea.

Teresa and I met Jenny one day by chance on the Palatine. She looked just the same, and greeted us with great gaiety, and said we must come to dinner one night.

Then life began again just as usual.

In November, Jane Sedley was back again in Rome, and Wilfrid Harris... He seemed to be on the best of terms with Jenny again. She was apparently leading just the same life as she had always led. Her flat was always full of people. She entertained. Adderly was in Rome. Gallazzi came back from Africa in December. She saw Charles, too, apparently ... everything was as it had been.

Godfrey saw her almost every day. I was puzzled. Teresa and I dined with Jenny, and we saw her quite often. She dined with us, and our relations were, on the surface, normal and comfortable. But ... there was something unsatisfactory somewhere.

I was longing (so I said to myself) to go back to England, but Jenny, on one of the few occasions when I had any talk to her, had said to me, 'You have not forgotten your promise? Remember, only one year. After that, do what you like.'

She did not look well, and I talked about this to Godfrey, who said to me:

'She isn't well, and the doctor at the Mont Dore, who is a very clever man, said she ought to take great care of herself. He says she is living on her nerves.'

She was certainly living a gay life, and every day, so I heard, and every night, she did something.

It was about Christmas-time that the next trifling event, which proved to be capital in the drama, occurred. The Zikovs were appointed to London.

Godfrey came to see me and told me the news, and he also told me that he was in a difficulty. He had meant to exchange into the Foreign Office for a time last year, but now it was too late. In the meantime he had unexpectedly been given this better post in Rome. The Zikovs, he said, were such old friends of his; they had always wanted him to be in

London if ever they were appointed to London. It had so nearly happened, but now it was frankly impossible. He could not, however much he wanted to, give up his post in Rome. It was impossible for him to exchange into the Foreign Office, however much he might want to, at this present moment.

'They don't understand this,' he said; 'they don't understand our service and how it is managed. They think that anything can be done through influence, but it really is impossible.'

When he said 'they', I knew it meant Vera Zikov. But Jane Sedley told me that Zikov, who was rather a commonplace, second-rate man, and who was jealous of everybody, had been so perfectly managed by Godfrey that he was no longer jealous of him, and that Godfrey had succeeded in giving everyone the necessary impression that he was friends with both of them.

'Godfrey is very clever,' Jane Sedley said to me, 'and has always managed the situation with consummate tact ... only I fear he has gone a little too far. I think he has over-reached himself.'

I asked her what she meant.

'Well,' she said, 'you see, he has used Jenny as a blind. Zikov thinks he is in love with

Jenny. He is always in her house and sees her every day. He's always there ... but, really, this is only done with Jenny's connivance, of course, for him to see Vera. It worked admirably at first, but now the Zikovs are going to London, and Vera, of course, wants Godfrey to go too. He won't. He says he can't, and I think it's true, but Vera sees clearly – or thinks she sees clearly – that he won't sacrifice his career or any step in his career for her; and she does not, firstly, believe in the difficulty; and, secondly, if she did, she would not be satisfied that regard for his career is a convincing and sufficient reason for his not going; she has been looking round for a reason that satisfies *her*, and she has found one.'

I asked what it was.

'Jenny,' said Jane. 'She has begun to think that Godfrey has been in love with Jenny all this time.'

'But surely that's absurd?'

Jane said that of course it was absurd, but nothing would be too absurd for Vera to believe if once she was jealous and got something like that into her head. The more absurd it was, the more firmly she would believe it. I said I supposed Godfrey would be clever enough to deal with the situation somehow, once he realized it.

160

Jane said she supposed so – if he realized it – but would he realize it?

I felt thankful that I was well out of the whole game. I considered that as far as I was concerned everything was over. The only black spot on the horizon was Charles. He would not come near us. We saw nothing of him and heard nothing of him. Jane had not set eyes on him either.

'He's still madly in love with Jenny,' she said, 'but you see, it's hopeless. Jenny has too many irons in the fire already. Her life is full to the brim. It is all she can do already to manage and deal with her ordinary people, without taking on artists and writers.'

Jane laughed knowingly.

'The best thing for *them,*' she said, 'is to fly away directly they feel that their wings have been singed in the flame, and, to do them justice, that is what they generally do.'

'But does she really care for anyone?' I asked.

'Jenny?' said Jane. 'She cares for *everybody.*'

That night I met Jenny at a small dinner given by some Americans. Godfrey was there, and the Zikovs. Jenny was gay, but I thought her gaiety forced, although I had no talk with her during dinner. Godfrey sat next to her and talked to her the whole time, and, remembering what Jane had said to me, I thought that Vera Zikov looked at Jenny with no good eye.

And then after dinner Godfrey said:

'Jenny, you must act for us.'

'Oh, not tonight, please, please not,' said Jenny.

'Oh, do,' said Godfrey. 'This is the last chance Countess Zikov will have of seeing you. Mustn't she do it?' he appealed to the Zikovs.

Zikov, a small, colourless man with a beard, said:

'Oh, yes, if you please!'

'Yes, *please* do,' said Countess Zikov, and there was, I thought, something ominous in the insinuating way she pleaded.

Jenny was talked round. She borrowed two shawls.

I had never seen her more graceful. I remembered the first time I had seen her do these 'poses', when Charles had been there. On this occasion she was still better – she excelled herself. First of all she was Daphne, and then Medea, and then a Maenad. She sketched a dance in which she was as light as a leaf and as graceful as a swan ... then she indicated the story of Orpheus and Eurydice.

Now Godfrey, where artistic things were

concerned, when he was faced with real art, when it occurs, which in our sullen, matter-of-fact world is all too rare, responded with a quickness and a sensitiveness and an enthusiasm that I have never seen equalled. He was, as the Germans say, 'out of himself' with joy and appreciation; he sat on the floor clapping his hands in ecstasy, and there were tears in his eyes when it was all over ... and Jenny flung herself down on a sofa, tired and exhausted...

Godfrey came up to her, and said:

'It's *wonderful* ... you are a wonderful woman, Jenny ... thank you so much ... it has been a glorious treat ... I shall never forget it ... never,' and his eyes filled with tears again.

Countess Zikov was looking at him and listening to every word he said. Jenny and Godfrey went into the next room, where there was a buffet. Jenny was thirsty, and wanted some lemonade.

'How clever she is!' Countess Zikov said to me, 'but I think the dance was perhaps a pity ... I think that is a little beyond her, perhaps that is because I am spoilt, being used to our ballet.'

'Of course,' I said, 'but, then, she doesn't pretend to dance ... it's only an indication.'

'Yes,' said Countess Zikov, 'but I find if

one dances that one *should* pretend to dance or else not dance at all.'

Then we had some music. Somebody played and someone else sang, and at one moment I found myself sitting next to Jenny in the next room. She had wanted a cigarette, and gone to get one, and I had followed her. While we were there a song had begun, and everyone else had gone back into the drawing-room, leaving us alone.

I told Jenny how much I had admired her 'poses'.

'Godfrey did,' she said, 'but did *you*?'

'With all my heart and soul,' I said; and this was true.

True, perfectly true, but I had also wondered at the time, how anyone so shallow, or whom I thought was so shallow as Jenny, could possibly manage to express so much serious and tragic beauty with such consummate art, considering she had had no training and not much education ... and no culture, and nothing serious in her.

'Well,' she said, 'you ought to have liked it, because I was doing it for *you* ... and for you only... I acted all I have never said to you, and I felt that perhaps you were understanding. You did understand a little?'

'Yes,' I said, 'I did understand.'

'This is the only way we can communicate now,' she said, smiling, 'but you know, of course, that nothing is changed, that I am just the same. I love you just as much as ever, and I always shall ... and you haven't changed?'

'No, I haven't changed.'

'And I shall never change ... never, never ... not even when I'm dead.' And suddenly an immense sadness passed over her face.

'You're not ill, are you, Jenny?' I asked.

'Not ill, very well in a way ... but incurable, all the same.' She laughed.

The music had come to an end in the next room.

'I think we had better go back,' she said.

We went back into the next room. Nobody noticed us.

There was a crowd of people talking and laughing. More guests had arrived. Supper was suggested, and we went into another room ... not the dining-room where the buffet had been, and sat down at little tables.

Godfrey sat between Countess Zikov and Jenny. I sat next to Jane Sedley.

Jenny left as soon as supper was finished. I thought she looked tired, and she was coughing a little.

She said good night to me as she passed

me ... I was talking to my American hostess ... and I shall remember the look in her eyes till my dying day.

That was the last time in my life that I ever exchanged a look or a meaning word with Jenny, and although we met again ... in one sense, in the real sense of the word, we never met again.

CHAPTER 12

Two days later the Zikovs left for London.

And then the day after I met Jane Sedley, who told me that Jenny had gone back to Naples.

'She is not well,' she said. 'Rome is too cold for her, but she has promised to come back for the Gallazzi's charity fête; that's in February, during the carnival. She has promised to do her "poses" at it ... it will be lovely. The Gallazzis have a wonderful house. It belongs now to Alfredo – since his father died – but his mother still lives there on the top floor.'

I asked if Jenny had gone by herself.

'She's gone by herself, but she will not be

alone for long. Wilfrid Harris is sure to go, and I shouldn't wonder if Alfredo went too ... he's more in love with her than when he went away.'

Godfrey came to see me the same day.

He was considerably perturbed. He had had a terrible scene with Vera Zikov. She had gone quite crazy, he said. She was wildly jealous of Jenny. Such jealousy was of course, he said, utterly baseless. I knew this was true. But Vera had refused to listen to reason, to listen at all.

She had suddenly seen red after the dinner at the Americans', and she had been to see Jenny. What had she done?

'I don't know what she did,' said Godfrey, 'but I am afraid she did something either mischievous or cruel. I tremble to think what. She wrote and told me she had been to see her. She refused to say goodbye to me. I went to see her off at the station ... there was a crowd of people, and she hardly took any notice of me at all ... and this is what happens after ten years' unwavering devotion. We had rows before, but never anything like this.'

Godfrey was almost in tears. I comforted him as best I could, and told him that directly Vera arrived in London she would be sorry, and all would be well.

'No,' he said, 'the truth is, she can't forgive me for not going to London, and she won't believe that it was impossible. She is convinced that Jenny prevented it. She won't understand that I have known Jenny ever since she was a child and that she is just like a sister to me. She never was jealous of Jenny before, but now she hates her with a savage hatred. I can't understand it.'

I was uneasy. What had Countess Zikov done to Jenny? What had she said or done?

The next day I got a letter from the Abbé asking me to go and see him, naming the day, at teatime, in his flat.

I obeyed his summons. He lived at the top floor of a large Palazzo. I found him welcoming and charming, as usual. He gave me a cup of tea and a brioche. When we had had our tea, he said to me:

'You are wondering why I have asked you to come and see me. I have been given a difficult duty to perform by Madame True. She has asked me to do what she says she cannot do herself.'

He paused.

I looked on the ground, wondering what he was going to say next.

'She came to see me,' he said, 'and made me various confidences, which, of course, will remain between her and me, and I am only telling you what I have the right to tell; but she asked me to tell you one thing which she said she could neither tell you nor write to you herself.'

He paused, and again I waited in silence.

The Abbé cleared his throat.

'She has guessed everything,' he said. 'She knows everything.'

'About what?' I asked.

'The comedy that has been played, and the reasons that inspired it.'

I said nothing.

'The laudable desire to save that young man. The comedy which you began to play insensibly by degrees, hardly knowing you were doing it ... determining, perhaps, again and again not to do it, or not to go on? Am I right? I believe, after you saw me and spoke about it, indirectly, that you decided not to do anything more. Alas! it was then already too late. You had already done too much! The comedy was half done – it was too late to go back. And then, perhaps, you thought she was playing a comedy as well. That you understood each other – *comme deux augures* ... am I right? That she was giving you the right answers to her cues... Alas! for the poor child it was never a comedy. It turned to drama at once, and now it is turning to tragedy. She loved you, my poor child. You have broken that love, and broken it for ever.'

'But I love *her*, Monsieur l'Abbé.'

I realized now in a blinding flash that this was true; that it had always been true, although I had only just realized it, and never realized it before.

Now an abyss seemed to have been opened at my feet. Everything was lit up as by a flash of lightning... I saw what I had never seen ... that I loved Jenny as I had never loved any-one ... not even Teresa ... that I was willing to throw away everything for her ... and not only that, but that I had lost her ... lost her for ever ... I had thrown the pearl away, richer than all my tribe.

'I love her,' I said, 'and now it's too late.'

'*Mon pauvre enfant,*' he said, 'you are quite right. It *is* too late.'

'But will she ever understand?' I asked.

'She does not blame you,' he said, after a time, 'not at all ... she understands why you did what you did, but you have broken a crystal vase that can never be mended ... all explanations would be useless. She already understands what there is to explain. It is the fact that you were able to do what you did. That you did it. The fact that you thought she was playing a comedy, too.'

'I did at first, but only at first.'

That was already too much.'

'And now?' I asked.

'I am afraid she may die of it.'

'Not *die?*'

'Yes, my poor child, *die*. She is of those who die.'

'Can I do nothing?'

'Nothing, nothing, nothing ... except ask *le Bon Dieu* to forgive you.'

'Monsieur l'Abbé, I don't believe in the *Bon Dieu*. I believe in a *Dieu*, but I agree with one of your writers who said that whoever created man must have been either very stupid or very cruel.'

'No doubt, *mon enfant*, and it is perhaps because you believed that that all this has happened.'

'But she doesn't know how much I love her,' I said. 'I did not know myself till today, till I saw you... Can't she know that?'

'*A quoi bon*, now?' he said. 'It's too late. That is the tragedy of life. Things happen too late, and once they are too late there is nothing to be done. You cannot force time to go backwards.'

'But, Monsieur l'Abbé, couldn't I go to

her and tell her everything ... if she understands she will understand that, and forgive
everything...?'

'And then?'

That was the question. What was to happen then?

'Do you think,' he went on, 'that she will
let you abandon your wife, whom she loves
and respects, and your son? Do you think
that if ever she had thought she might do
this, she would do it now? And would you
wish her to do it? *Elle ne vous aime plus, mon
cher enfant, mais elle est capable d'en ourir.*'

I said I understood, and I asked him
whether he could not explain everything to
her.

'I have done that already,' he said; 'she
understands everything, but she can't undo
what you have done.'

I said I had been blind from the start, but
it was not only conceit and vanity that had
blinded me, it was not only self-love, it was
self-depreciation, too ... I could not believe
at the time that she could really love me ...
and then I deceived myself ... and I had
thought she was 'light'...

'*Oui, elle est légère,*' said the Abbé. '*Elle
montera au ciel plus facilement;* she has a soul
as delicate as gossamer, but *dur comme un*

rubis ... she is like her mother in that. I knew her, too. *Une âme d'élite.'*

I asked the Abbé what there was to be done.

'You know the only advice I can give you,' he said, 'is advice you will not take.'

'Is remorse a sin?' I asked him.

'No,' he said. 'Remorse is salutary, unless it is pushed beyond the verge of despair. Despair is a sin, and final despair the greatest of sins.'

'What can I do then? I can't even pray.'

'I will pray for you ... as for you, you must try and live for others. One never knows; perhaps all this which seems at the moment to be so cruel and so irremediable and so senseless is in reality one of the means the *Bon Dieu* is using to lead you into a better way. I do not wish to preach to you, *mon enfant.* Let it be enough for you that I am sorry for you. *Allons, mon enfant, du courage.'*

I left him and went for a long walk by myself in the streets of Rome. I understood what had happened. Godfrey had told the whole story as I had told it him at Naples to Vera Zikov, and she in her rage, and from a wish to wound, and out of jealousy, had repeated it to Jenny. I was not angry with Godfrey. I should never reproach him with it. It was my fault, not his. I should never have told him the story, and, what was more, I should never have let the story happen.

The Abbé was right. There was no question of explanation or forgiveness. Jenny knew now exactly what had happened, and however much I might love her, and however well and fully she might realize that I loved her *now*, I could not undo what I had done. I had shattered the crystal vase. I had broken the bowl of her love to pieces. I had trampled the pearl underfoot. Oh! if one could only put back the clock...! If only those days could be lived over again! Despair was a sin, the Abbé said, and my remorse was desperate ... however, the only thing to be done now was to try and prevent Teresa from suffering. She must never know. Was there some comfort there? None.

Never know? She probably did know already. Two lines of poetry which I had learnt in the nursery kept on buzzing in my head:

'Oh! what a tangled web we weave
When first we practise to deceive.'

Especially when first we practise to deceive *ourselves!*

And then I thought to myself: 'After all,

was it too late?' Supposing I went to Jenny now, and said, 'Let the past be past; let us admit that what I did was abominable; what does it matter if I love you, if I have loved you all the time, and love you now?'

But she could no longer love me now, never any more; even if she did love me still ... nothing could mend the broken fragments of what had been. No, there was nothing to be done. I seemed to know Jenny now for the first time. I suppose I had known her before, known her all the time ... but I had deliberately blinded myself ... I refused to see her, or anything, as things really were...

The truth was, I now saw, that I had been in love with her all the time, from the very first moment; but I had refused to admit it, refused to see it. I had deceived myself from the start to the finish. I had thought to deceive Jenny, but it was only myself that I had deceived. I had said to myself, 'Jenny is playing a comedy and I must join in, I must play up.' Even looking back at this moment I realized, I think I realized what I *now* am certain of, that at the very moment when I spoke of Jenny's comedy and game, in my heart of hearts, I knew that it was not true.

That, on the contrary, it was *I* who was playing a game, a comedy, and that I enjoyed playing it. I enjoyed playing it because I was in love with Jenny, and I refused to face the fact; refused to see that the comedy might turn to drama, even after the Abbé had pointed out the danger to me. What I had suffered from, from beginning to end, was self-deception. I had cheated myself.

Godfrey had been right when he had said to me that what had begun in the friendship for a man, had grown without my knowing it into a violent passion for a woman ... that otherwise my mania for saving Charles was inexplicable ... it *was* inexplicable. Charles had been an excuse – a pretext. I had never thought Charles was really in danger. I had never really cared if he was. He had not been in danger. The only danger that he ran was the danger I was running the risk of creating myself. Jenny might well out of jealousy have aimed at capturing him for good, as the Abbé said ... she had *not* done that (not deliberately), because she never had cause for jealousy, as she thought ... no more she had ... and now Charles accused me of not knowing Jenny ... of having ruined Jenny's life as well as his life ... and that was true.

Charles' work? Charles would go on working. If not now, later; he was young; he was full of life and sap; he would get over this, however much he might be suffering *now* but my work, I felt, was done for forever. This would kill all the small creative impulse I had.

How could I begin to invent fictitious dramas and crises and psychological situations in the face of the overwhelming reality? How could I think of inventing a heroine when the shadow of Jenny would ever be before me, and with Teresa by my side? Jenny and Teresa! Two avenging angels!

By this time I had reached the Santa Trinità dei Monti. The sun was setting over Rome. The upper air was crystal clear and cold. In the west there was a bar of scarlet surmounted by a broad belt of velvet mouselike grey cloud fringed with a rim of wintry fire.

The Dome of St Peter's shone like a sombre beryl stone. Bells were ringing. The people who were strolling on the hill were dark in the sunset, muffled in cloaks ... the cypress trees were black and sharp against the pale luminous east... It was the hour when people said in old times it was unhealthy to be out of doors in Rome ... some people were hurrying home, but already they knew too much about malaria and its real causes to be frightened of the sunset... I stood against the wall and watched.

Lights were twinkling, there was an indescribable discordant melody in the air, and the smell of centuries... 'Nothing,' I thought, 'can ever spoil Rome. Nothing comes amiss here. Nothing matters, neither posters, nor advertisements, nor trams, nor modern buildings; it all fits in. Does everything fit in ... in time? One thing is certain.

'Art and the writing of ephemeral books does not matter, and I have spoilt my life so far by thinking such things mattered, and that only such things mattered. Sometimes a great writer here and there will be made the mouthpiece of the Divine, and speak a message that will echo for a few moments through the corridors of time ... but for the rest, they are as short-lived as flies.'

At that moment I heard the strident, greedy cries of the newsvendors shouting their evening wares – 'as ephemeral', I thought, 'as those news-sheets... Life is stronger than art. Good art can only come, the Abbé once said to me, from good living.'

My art had become bad because my life had become bad. 'But then whose life was good?' and a mocking voice suggested that artists were bad but art was good.

The truth seemed to come to me with the

voice of the bells. The Abbé had told me to keep art and life in their proper categories; to render to art what was due to art, and to life what was due to life. Art was a part of life, and good art was a part of good life. I had disputed this. I had thought that art had nothing to do with life and mattered far more than morals. That in Charles' case I did not care a fig for his morals, but I was determined to save his art.

I thought I would save him from Jenny and show him that he was playing with fire.

The Abbé had said I was all wrong, that life would prove too strong for me, would recoil and get back on me.

I had not listened and had gone ahead with my plan, and I had burnt myself at the fire. I had fallen into the pit from which I had hoped to save Charles. The result was it was *my* art that had perished.

Was the Abbé right? Had it perished because good art is the result of good life? Was this true of *all* artists and all art? Was their work always affected by their lives? Was what was good in their art the reflection of what was good in their lives? Were their faults as artists the result of flaws in their character and their conduct?

I had always thought the opposite; that art

was quite independent of life and morals, and separate from them, and blew where it listed.

But now I reflected: is anything in the universe separate from anything else? Nobody's life is wholly good, because nobody is wholly good; and nobody's art is wholly good. The greatest men, the greatest lives and achievements, are comparative failures. Sometimes, the greater the man, the greater the failure; witness Napoleon. And is it some flaw in the character that reacts on the art? Did Harriet's drowned body perhaps prevent Shelley from finishing so much? Did Lili's broken heart and shattered life account for the imperfections of Faust and help to chill so much of Goethe's work? Did some unknown quantity of misery and passion (some tremendous X) perhaps come between Shakespeare and his vision? Between Shakespeare and his artistic satisfaction? Between what he did and what he knew he could or might have done as an artist? For if Shakespeare's plays were the dead ashes of his inspiration, what must the live coal of his vision have been? Perhaps plays were to him what reporting in the House of Commons was to Dr Johnson and Dickens. Perhaps he loathed the stage, and he certainly hated the 'public means which public manners breeds'.

And then I thought, this is neither paradox nor the biassed utterance of a religious official, nor the ravings of a crank. Translated into other terms, it is a commonplace: *'Le style c'est l'homme même.'* We all know, for instance, that Byron was a genius, and we all know that the work of Byron is marred and sometimes ruined by egotism and affectation; the sincerity and the truth in it break in from time to time like rifts of sunshine on a murky day; and the same thing is true of how many? Surely of all authors and artists – only one or two of them in the whole history of the world seem *to us* complete, like whole fine days: Homer, Dante and Shakespeare ... (not even Goethe).

In the case of these great men and these great achievements, and of men less great, but still great, even their acknowledged failures, let alone their comparative failures (their successes), are huge and imposing; their most fragmentary achievements are at least a part of the dreams of mankind. But lesser men leave lesser things; and in my case, my art was certainly too small and too weak a thing to survive the shock and the infection it suffered and caught from the fever which had stricken my life. My life might recover, but my art would never recover; it would be ephemeral as today's newspaper ... and I had brought this all about and more – ah! how much more! in the name of Art ...

Then the sun set; the fires faded from the sky, and I went home.

CHAPTER 13

Our life resumed its normal course. Teresa and I led a retired life. I was supposed to be working. Charles, I heard, was working and had finished a picture, a portrait of an old American lady he had just done for money. It is the celebrated picture of Mrs S– that now hangs in the Luxembourg.

I sometimes heard news of Jenny from Jane Sedley. She said Jenny was leading a full, gay life, as usual. I sometimes saw the Abbé, but he never referred to anything that had happened.

In February, Jenny came back to Rome. I felt she had arrived before I heard the news, or rather before I saw it announced in the *New York Herald*. She had come back for the charity fête.

I heard of the rehearsals.

The fête was the topic of all Roman tea parties and dinner parties, and the cause of much heart-burning. Some people objected to Jenny's taking part in it, 'but as it was for charity...' they said... One or two famous professionals were going to appear. Madame Clara Voce, an old lady who had retired a long time ago from the stage, had promised to read a passage from Dante, Zechetti, the great actress, was going to recite, and Giraldi, the prima donna, was to sing.

Other people said it was conceited of Jenny to appear with all these professionals. It was all very well to pose in a drawing-room before friends, but she was, after all, an amateur.

Teresa and myself had been asked to be patrons, and we had accepted. There was no longer now any question of my incognito at Rome, but no more was there much question of my notoriety.

The *Silver Pound* had already been supplanted by something newer and more popular, and Roman society had never heard of my more serious work.

Charles, I heard, was designing some of the costumes. There was to be, besides music and recitations, a masque called *Orpheus and Eurydice*, arranged by Bonselmi, in which

Jenny was to play a leading part. She had suggested the idea to him. It was in pantomime. She was also going to do a dance. People said this was too audacious, as it was well-known that, graceful as she was, she was not a dancer.

But Jenny, I heard from Godfrey, was taking a feverish interest in the rehearsals and, besides that, she was leading the gayest of lives, hunting in the Campagna and sitting up late every night.

I did not believe any longer in the reality of this gaiety. I was not deceived by it.

I was not now going to make any more mistakes in psychology.

The fête was coming off in the evening on the Thursday in carnival week at the Palazzo Gallazzi. No better setting could have been chosen. The rooms were spacious and high. They had faded red silk on the walls, dark pictures and beautiful crystal chandeliers.

People said it was a scandal that Gallazzi should have asked Jenny to perform while his mother was still alive; but Princess Gallazzi had signified her intention of being present, so whispering tongues were silenced on that score.

Two or three days before the performance, I had a visit from Godfrey Law, who said to me that he thought Jenny was burning the candle at both ends, and that if she was not careful she would have a breakdown. 'She hunts or rehearses all day,' he said, 'and she dances or rehearses all night. She will kill herself if she goes on like this.' Couldn't I do anything to stop it? But I explained to Godfrey that I was so busy now that I never went out, and that I had not set eyes on Jenny for weeks. This was true, but we did meet once before the performance.

It was in St Peter's.

Teresa and I strolled into the church one morning early, and at one of the side altars we saw Jenny kneeling. She was dressed in black. Jenny had never been particularly religious, and I wondered whether she was there on account of some particular anniversary. She got up as we were walking in, and as she passed us she stopped, and said 'How do you do?' in a friendly way. She talked to both of us together.

'I shall have to fly,' she said, 'because I have got to rehearse.'

Teresa asked how it was going.

Jenny laughed and shrugged her shoulders...

'It's awful,' she said, 'they all quarrel the whole time ... we're not certain of *any* of the stars. Each one says he or she won't act unless his or her name is in the biggest print. Madame Clara Voce is so old that they say it will kill her ... besides which she forgets her lines, although she has a book in her hand. She can't see to read. It is doubtful whether Zechetti will appear at all, and she refuses to come to any rehearsal ... altogether, I expect it will be a terrible failure. However, one must go through with it.'

'And your performance?' said Teresa.

'Oh, mine doesn't matter. I'm doing a dance ... it's called "Autumn Leaves" ... and I've got the most lovely clothes ... designed by Charles Donne...' she smiled, quite naturally, 'and then there's the masque *Orpheus and Eurydice.*'

Teresa said she supposed Jenny was doing Eurydice.

'No,' said Jenny, 'oddly enough I'm doing Orpheus. It's absurd, isn't it? I was cast for Eurydice at first, and then we couldn't get an Orpheus. We tried a young man, and we tried an old woman, and we tried a boy, and none of them could do it. And then we tried a professional actress ... and Bonselmi, who had invented the whole thing, tore his hair out, and he's got very long hair and a lot of it. When he saw me rehearsing my part as

Eurydice, he made me try Orpheus, and apparently he was satisfied – at any rate he wouldn't hear of anyone else doing it. They were all huffy at first, but he became obstinate, and so there it was.'

I asked who was to do Eurydice.

'Alfredo Gallazzi's sister,' she said, 'she is quite young, and a dream of beauty... She has really little to do because she is veiled most of the time, but she has got to move ... and she moves like a flower in the wind. It will be worth seeing for that. And Donna Laura does Proserpine ... sitting on a throne dressed in black with a wreath of poppies. She looks wonderful. Now I must go.'

These were her last words, and the last words I ever heard her speak.

When she left us, I said to Teresa that I thought she was looking very well, which was true.

'I have never seen her look so well,' said Teresa, 'as far as *looks* are concerned, but she is looking far *too* well ... a flame that is burning what is round it to ashes.'

I said I supposed it was the fête and the rehearsals.

Teresa agreed.

'But you see,' Teresa said more to herself than to me, 'Jenny is one of those people who are *"aus Yemen"*.'

I asked what on earth she meant.

Teresa laughed. 'You have forgotten your Heine,' she said, 'I was thinking of one of his romances. I think it is called *Der Asra*, but I forget... I don't know why I thought of it at that minute, but I meant that Jenny was one of those people who give their heart and soul to whatever they are doing in the same absolute way Mohammedans do ... the poem is about a Mohammedan ... even if this fête were killing her, she would put every drop of her blood, every ounce and inch of her will, and every nerve in her body into it.'

I laughed and said a fête wasn't as bad as all that. After all, she would have a rest in Lent.

'Yes,' said Teresa, 'she will have a rest in Lent.'

CHAPTER 14

Then came the night of the performance. Teresa and I dined with Godfrey. There was no one else there, but Jane Sedley. Godfrey was excited about the fête, and told us amusing stories about what had been happening.

There had been quarrels right up to the last, and it was doubtful even now whether some of the leading performers would not throw up their parts at the last moment.

We arrived early; we had good seats, the middle of the fourth row.

Jane went behind the scenes to see Jenny, and other friends of hers.

She came back with a face of consternation.

'The worst has happened,' she said, 'Jenny has not turned up.'

'Oh!' said Godfrey, 'whoever else may throw over, *she* won't; she's late. She always is late.'

'No, it's not that,' said Jane. 'She went out hunting today ... hunting, if you please, on the day of the performance, and she's not back ... and she's not at her flat.'

Godfrey was calm. 'She told me,' he said, 'she was going to have a ride in the Campagna. She said she had rehearsed enough ... that it would clear her brain.'

'Yes,' said Jane, 'but the point is, the whole thing begins in ten minutes, and she is not here. She may have had an accident.'

'No,' said Godfrey, calmly, 'I think she's late. You see, her turns are not till later.'

There was, among a certain group of the

people who had been responsible for getting up the whole thing, a buzz of conversation, otherwise the rest of the audience were unconscious that anything untoward had happened.

The curtain went up, rather late.

It is a curious thing that, although I should have thought every detail of that performance would have been branded on my mind for ever, and although many details of it *are* branded on my mind, there are large slabs of it, as it were ... that I have forgotten.

I remember the overture: played by an amateur orchestra. They all wore blue ribbons like an order, and they were all dressed in white silk. The conductor was an English lady.

They played very nicely. But behind me there was a dear old *Musik-Direktor* Lang, a German, and he said to me:

'But, no.'

Then I remember, I don't think it came next, a play in one act, by Musset; *Il faut qu'une porte soit ouverte ou fermée;* two members of the French Embassy acted in it. It was, I think, acted well. It was greatly applauded. I don't think I paid much attention to it. But I remember a charming passage in it about 'l'Amour' being 'une comédie' 'l'Amour est mort, vive l'Amour!' and that passage went to my heart.

I had reason to know something about the comedy of love... And then what came next... I remember an interminable solo on the pianoforte which was encored, and the pianist played, as an encore, a tune from a ballet called *Sylvia*, by Délibes.

The players in the orchestra smiled to one another when he played this. They had played it so often themselves, and knew it so well.

There was no interval, and the time came for Jenny's dance.

Evidently there had been a change in the programme, for instead of the dance, Madame Clara Voce came on to the stage dressed in brown, her grey hair parted in the middle.

'Jenny has not come back,' Jane said to us, in a frightened whisper.

But we paid no attention. Madame Clara Voce held a book in her hand. She read the passage about Paolo and Francesca from the *Inferno*. Her voice was low, and beautiful, so was her expression, and the audience went wild. They clapped as only an Italian audience can clap.

After that there was an anticlimax ... I

forget what it was.

Then someone made an announcement that Madame Zechetti had been prevented from appearing owing to a serious head-ache, and the announcement was followed by a murmur of resigned disappointment.

After a slight pause, Giraldi, the prima donna, appeared on the stage.

In spite of being a prima donna, she was unaffected, and unselfconscious. She talked to the accompanist, hummed the tune to him, beat a bar of the time to him on the pianoforte, and I heard the words *Si, caro,* said in such a tone that they in themselves were worth coming to hear.

Then she looked at the accompanist a second, and began to sing. She sang a song from the *Traviata,* and I remembered being only conscious of her dark eyes that seemed to say, 'But what wrong have I done to *you?'* I felt as if I alone in that audience were responsible for that unfathomable suffering, that immitigable pain.

Once more there was a tornado of applause, and the audience was delirious.

She was encored, of course. I wondered what she was going to sing. She sang a poem of Victor Hugo's that I'd heard sung a thou-sand times, set to what musicians tell me is a commonplace amateurish tune, composed by a baroness (as if that mattered).

'*Si vous n'avez rien à me dire.*' Was it commonplace? Was it good? Was it bad? I don't know, and I cared still less. All that I knew was that a soul bared and naked seemed to be talking to me. It was *Jenny* talking to *me*. It was myself, what was now my dead but eternal self talking to Jenny, to her dead but eternal self.

Was the whole concert conspiring to touch me on the raw? Everything, I thought, applies to everybody. If you look out a phrase in the Bible or in Shakespeare, the line you strike on is always exactly appropriate to the person who looks it out. That is the reason perhaps of the inevitable rightness of the *Sortes Virgilianae*. And now Giraldi was talking to me. The fact of her being a genius, or the song being a poor song, was neither here nor there. Not that the words or the music were in themselves particularly appropriate ... *it was the whole thing.* It was Giraldi's singing, her phrasing, her looks: I thought she was singing for me, to me, at me, and about Jenny.

'*Si vous n'avez rien à me dire,*
Pourquoi venir auprès de moi?

193

Pourquoi me faire ce sourire
Qui tournerait la tête au roi?
Si vous n'avez rien à me dire.
Pourquoi venir auprès de moi?'

'Why? Why? Why? Jenny, did you ever come into my life? If you had nothing to say to me?' But was it not rather she who would be justified in saying that to me? It was I who had forced my way into her life, when I had had nothing to say to her ... *then.*

'Si vous n'avez rien à m'apprendre,
Pourquoi me pressez-vous la main?
Sur le rêve angèlique et tendre,
Auquel vous songez en chemin,
Si vous n'avez rien à m'apprendre,
Pourquoi me pressez-vous la main?'

Might not Jenny have well said that to me? The voice of conscience and doom, and retribution, seemed to be talking to me from the grave. From the *grave?* I shivered. Supposing Jenny...

'Si vous voulez que je m'en aille,
Pourquoi passez-vous par ici?
Lorsque je vous vois je tressaille,
C'est ma joie et c'est mon souci.

194

Si vous voulez que je m'en aille,
Pourquoi passez-vous par ici?'

But Jenny, it was *you*, who told me not to go! May I not well say that to you? I might have said 'yes', but not *now*. I had forfeited that right. I knew that all too well.

The song stopped; there was shouting, and flowers, and stamping: an ovation.

I forget what happened next.

Then I remember Jane saying: 'I wonder whether Jenny has turned up. Shall I go and see?'

But Godfrey dissuaded her. There wasn't time, and it was too difficult. If everything hadn't been all right, we should have known by now. There came some other item, I forget what, and then the curtain went up on *Orpheus and Eurydice:* a pantomime with music.

I say the curtain went up, but I think there was probably an overture – I didn't heed it. I remember the curtain going up. The stage was dim. There was a chant sung by a chorus, in the distance, and then Eurydice was carried in on her funeral bier strewn with white flowers, and veiled.

There was a sound of flutes and a high monotonous wail; a vision of veiled figures.

The procession seemed to march through valleys of a springtide that had suddenly been darkened by sorrow: an April day veiled all at once by a fugitive storm.

Orpheus came on, and waved the mourners away, and he sat down by the corpse of Eurydice. He wanted to be alone with his grief.

Jane and Godfrey gave a sigh of relief. It *was* Jenny ... yes, it was Jenny, but a Jenny that I had never known and never seen, never guessed of, not even when she had been at her best, doing her 'poses'.

The majesty of grief was about her, and the desolation of bereavement, stretching far away like the sands from a ruin in the desert.

She was almost motionless.

She once lifted the veil from Eurydice's features, and then she let it drop quickly, as if she had touched a burning iron. She shivered from the incandescent wound, and then she sat down again, and looked into space, which seemed to grow wider and larger and more desolate about her.

Hers was the grief which is too great for words: the grief which cannot be unpacked in tears or released in cries. It was mute and immutable and lasting: πένθος ἄλαστον. (Comfortless sorrow).

You could have heard a pin drop in the audience. And then, without looking back at the bier, she walked away into the distance, into the dim opalescent meadows up a high path. She had turned her back on us, but oh! the expression of irremediable grief, of unutterable sorrow!

The curtain went down, but nobody clapped.

The music went on. I believe it was beautiful; but I didn't listen. The curtain went up again.

We were now in the Halls of Hell.

On two thrones, facing us, there was a stately Pluto, and Donna Laura Bartolini as Proserpine. She was dressed in black, with a scarlet coronal.

Jenny was there, kneeling, and afterwards standing with her back turned to us, but with her little head raised high, and her exquisite arms bare and outstretched.

There was a passion of entreaty in her pose; an ecstasy of supplication that must have moved stones.

Proserpine buried her head in her hands, and the actor who played Pluto (I have forgotten who he was) simulated the iron tears...

Slowly from the shadows Eurydice advanced, veiled, and Pluto led her to Orpheus, and she unveiled; young and radiant.

Orpheus opened wide his arms, and clasped Eurydice with a rapture, so swift that it happened before you knew it had happened, and with a joy so piercing that it cut you like a knife. The curtain went down.

There was more music. The curtain went up again on Hades: the halfway house to earth: a twilight of greens and sea blues. Soft emerald and muffled opal, diminished sapphire and drowned sunlight. Orpheus was showing Eurydice the way, happy and resolute. Eurydice was following, fearful and trembling, and yet glad. The whole thing only took a few moments, but it seemed to last an eternity.

The suspense was intolerable. *'Why don't they get on?'* one thought. 'They will spoil it all if they are not more careful and quicker. What is there to bother about?'

'Oh! Eurydice tell him, tell him not to look round. You are so nearly there.'

There was a shaft of light through the shadows, like the dawn quivering on a morning tide ... just a faint hint of the coming sunrise. Surely they had got there? Surely it was all right now? ... and then...

Before it happened, we knew it had

happened ... that it must happen. We could tell from Orpheus' back that he could not bear it a second longer...

'Now, he's done it ... we knew he would.'

A sharp sudden turn, a flash of blinding joy and then... She was going; she had gone; she melted into the shadows, she was one with the twilight; and as she went she seemed to leave a trail of moonlight behind her. Was it her veil? or just the reflection of the distant lights of the palace of Hades?

Now there was nothing. Only Orpheus alone in the gloom... And he looked at us, stricken to death, but not dead and not dying; and raising both hands, he walked away into the night.

The curtain went down, and the applause went on for at least five minutes. They called and screamed and stamped, and whistled and shouted and yelled. Bonselmi came on; Donna Laura came on; Eurydice came on, and there were still louder calls for Orpheus.

Then, when silence was restored, Bonselmi came on in front of the curtain and explained that the Signora True was indisposed.

'I will go to her at once,' said Jane. 'You wait here for me.'

I could see she was more than anxious, frightened.

We did not have to want long, but by the time she came back, the long high room was nearly empty. When Jane did come back to us, she was white in the face and desperately calm.

'She's dead,' she said, 'Jenny's dead … there's nothing to be done. And something extraordinary and mysterious has happened. When they went up to her dressing-room just now, they found her lying on a small sofa, *in her habit and riding boots*. She had not touched her Orpheus clothes, so she must have died before the play began.'

CHAPTER 15

The mystery was never cleared up, nor was it even much talked about; although later it filtered into life and became a well-known ghost story and a 'piece' for raconteurs; only a few people knew the facts. The doctor said Jenny had died before the performance, and when he was told at what time the performance took place, he simply said we had been mistaken.

If she had acted, the performance must

have taken place sooner, and she must for some reason have put on her riding clothes afterwards.

The other people who knew about it said the doctor was mistaken. She *had* acted, and put on her riding clothes to go home. What else could she have put on? She had died afterwards.

But the maid who was looking after the theatrical dresses was positive that Jenny's Orpheus dress had not been touched. The hall porter said he remembered her coming in, in her riding clothes, but he was vague about the time.

She had gone up by the small staircase straight to her dressing-room. She always did that at rehearsal and knew the way. Nobody had seen her till the moment came for the curtain to go up on Orpheus. She had then appeared in the wings ready for her cue.

There was nothing odd about this, as everybody was busy. There was a crowd of people behind the scenes. When the call-boy went for her she was there ready. She had not been in the Palazzo when she should have done her dance, and that number was cut out. Nobody spoke to her, and she spoke to no one.

Her death was attributed to heart failure,

brought on by overexcitement.

She was buried in Rome and there were many people at the funeral. The Abbé officiated. Charles was there, and he came up to me in the cemetery when it was over, and said, 'You killed Jenny.'

I never saw him again to speak to, or except in the distance. He never wrote to me; he always cut me dead.

That is all there is to tell.

Teresa and I went back to London for Easter in time for the holidays.

I saw the Abbé several times. He was wonderful; he did not make one single reproach, but he knew what I felt, and he was sorry.

I told him about Charles, and asked him whether he thought his artistic career and his life would be ruined.

He thought not ... he thought his art might possibly gain from what he'd been through, but he would, he thought, be very unhappy for a time. He certainly was unhappy for a long time; but his art did not suffer.

I told him what Charles had said to me.

The Abbé said no human being had the right to judge me or anyone. It was an affair between me and God.

Then we left Rome and went to London. I began another book in place of the one I had given up – a serious book. I was able to finish it after a time. It came out two years later, and it was not a success.

The critics said it was a disappointment, and the public endorsed their view.

The year after we left Rome, Charles exhibited the first picture that made him really famous. It was better than anything he had done hitherto. His success was then assured, and he went on from strength to strength as everyone knows: but he is still unmarried.

My literary career came to an end, although I am at this moment well-known for other reasons in another department of life. I have done well. I have been a 'success'. There are initials after my name, and my letters to *The Times* are printed in large print. Many people do not even know that I am the author of a few books which were once well thought of, still less that I had anything to do with the *Silver Pound*. That, as a book, is forgotten. You can still buy it in the Tauchnitz, or at secondhand bookshops for ten shillings, and that price is owing to the illustrations, which are by de Lisle.

All that the *Silver Pound* produced, too, in the way of music has suffered eclipse, but it is not altogether forgotten.

The other night I was at a play, and during

the entracte, the orchestra played a tune that seemed familiar to me, although I could not place it.

My neighbour seemed to know it, and I asked him what it was.

'Oh,' he said, 'that is from an old operetta called *The Silver Pound*. It is quite forgotten now, but I remember it used to be very popular: Violet Lester used to sing in it.'

I asked him who it was by.

'Oh,' he said, 'Baudry, a Frenchman.'

'And who wrote the words?'

'I don't know,' he said. 'Nobody ever bothered about the words ... it was the usual rubbish, tosh, like most operettas, but the music was charming.'

I think the public was right to forget my works. I do not think they will ever be 're-discovered'. They were temporal and local, and perhaps served their purpose. I do not think I have been unfairly treated by fashion or fortune. Whenever the public or the critics agree with an author in the estimate of his work, he thinks they are right; whenever they disagree, he thinks he is the victim of a con-spiracy; in my case there was no conspiracy. My books were too well written (in one sense) and not well enough written (in another) to last. The *Silver Pound* was, after all, the best thing I ever did, and here again the public was right! But, right or wrong, what did it and what does it matter? What was the shipwreck of my art compared with that other devastation, the ruin of my life, that empty desert with its one permanent pyramid of remorse?

Teresa and I never alluded to Jenny. Nor can I even now speak of her and of all that. I think Teresa understood that – and everything.

When Teresa died a good many years after the events which I have related, I sold my London house and moved into a small flat. My son was married.

When I was packing, sorting the books and throwing things away, I came across a little volume of Heine's poems, called *Romanzero*.

I turned over the leaves casually, and came across a poem called 'Der Asra'.

I read it and remembered Teresa having quoted me a phrase from it one day when we were talking about Jenny in Rome. This was the stanza she had quoted from:

'Und der Sklave sprach: 'Ich heisse
Mohamed, Ich bin aus Yemen,
Und mein Stamm sind jene Asra,
Welche sterben wenn sie lieben.'

'Lady,' said the slave, 'My name is
   Mohamed
I am from Yemen;
And I am of the race of Asra,
Who die when they love.'

The stanza was underlined, and dated
'Rome, 18–'

I hadn't quite understood what Teresa had
meant when she quoted the phrase and said
that Jenny was *'aus Yemen'*, not even after
she had explained.

I understand now...

Vanderbilt Hotel New York, 19–.

The publishers hope that this book has given you enjoyable reading. Large Print Books are especially designed to be as easy to see and hold as possible. If you wish a complete list of our books please ask at your local library or write directly to:

Dales Large Print Books
Magna House, Long Preston,
Skipton, North Yorkshire.
BD23 4ND

This Large Print Book, for people
who cannot read normal print,
is published under the auspices of

THE ULVERSCROFT FOUNDATION